A Squad of Earth Police deployed themselves to prevent the Spacers from regaining their ships, but with the girls as hostages the raiders were safe from gunfire

"There Goes Anoth

Across the way th
and the Space ...d
into a ball of ... ompan-
ions dashed for ... n girls on
their shoulders. Bu ... ed off the metal
promenade.

Ben measured the distance to his own ship, then rolled the valuable earthgirl off his shoulder and held her like a shield as he ran. With the last of his strength he hoisted her up into the hatchway and climbed in behind.

IT WAS ONLY THEN THAT HE SAW THE YOUNG EARTHMAN INSIDE *THE SHIP, AIMING AN AUTOMATIC AT HIS CHEST FROM ACROSS THE CABIN. . . .*

RAIDERS FROM THE RINGS

A Science-Fiction Novel by

ALAN E. NOURSE

PYRAMID BOOKS
NEW YORK, N. Y.

RAIDERS FROM THE RINGS

A PYRAMID BOOK—Published by arrangement with David McKay Company, Inc.

PRINTING HISTORY

David McKay edition published April 1962
Pyramid edition published November 1963
Second printing, January 1965

Printed in the United States of America

Library of Congress Catalog Card No. 61-8729

PYRAMID BOOKS are published by Pyramid Publications, Inc., 444 Madison Avenue, New York 22, New York, U.S.A.

PROLOGUE

THE RAIDERS could hear the mauki's chant from the moment they boarded the ship from Earth.

It came from somewhere deep in the heart of the craft, and they paused as soon as the outer hatchway had been forced, listening in spite of themselves in the darkness of the corridor. It came to them softly at first: a clear, sweet woman's voice, sharp as crystal in their ears. Then it rose higher, mournful and shattering, and the words became distinct in the ancient, heart-rending lament that the raiders had heard so many times before. Urgent as their mission was, they could not help but listen for a moment, feeling the wave of sadness and longing surging up in their throats.

Beyond them the ship's corridor was empty; there was no sound here other than the chant. Not even the throbbing of the ship's generators was audible in the blackness. The raiders stood transfixed for a moment. Then Petro, the leader, took a deep breath and flicked on the battle lantern at his belt.

"She's here, all right," he said. "She must have the whole crew listening. Let's go."

The three men moved down the corridor, flashing their lights cautiously. Petro pointed to an overhead conduit. "Jack, that must be the main power cable. Follow it down to the generators, and wait for the word. Tiny, you come with me. And be careful. We can't assume that *everybody's* listening to the woman."

Silently they moved along to a corridor crossing, then ducked down a ladder into a storage hold. It had been ridiculously simple to break into this huge, clumsy ship from Earth. From the first fleeting contact a week before, the raiders had been stalking it, watching with contempt as it moved ponderously on its way through the Asteroid Belt, unaware that it had even been spotted. Finally it moved into the shadow of a huge chunk of asteroid debris and waited, obviously depending on its radar screens to pick up any approaching vessel. With the clumsiness so typical of Earthborn men in space, the crew of the Earth ship had overlooked the fact that the asteroid they were using for concealment was blinding them completely on one side.

It was then that the Spacer ship had moved in on its prey. Now the raiders were aboard, and the mauki was doing her part. Petro and Tiny worked their way through the pitch-black holds into the galley and down toward the brig area. They were big, powerful men but they moved like jungle cats in the darkness. Not once did they encounter one of the Earth crewmen. When they finally approached the brightly lighted mess hall just above the brig area, they saw the reason why.

The crew were listening to the mauki. The mess hall was crowded with men; still others were jamming the approach corridors and ladders down to the woman's cell. Some smoked, some munched slowly on the remnants of dinner, shifting to new positions for comfort, but all of them were listening intently to the haunting measures of the chant, like men in a dream from which they could not escape.

In her tiny cell in the brig, the mauki stood gripping the bars, a tall, straight, proud woman, filling her lungs and throwing her head back as she sang.

Entranced, her captors had become captives, straining to hear her, drawn from all quarters of the ship, leaving their work to come closer as the chant struck home. Petro winked at his companion, and ducked down a side corridor leading to the brig area. "She's got them hooked, all right," he said. "The child must be in there with her. Got the cutting torch ready?"

"Yes. But I don't see the kid."

Petro clicked on a handset. "Ready, Jack?"

"All set."

"Then let it blow."

Abruptly, the power went off, plunging the mess hall into darkness. The same instant, the mauki stopped her singing, and the crewmen's dream turned into a nightmare. Petro and Tiny dashed across into the brig, remembering landmarks, and dodged down the corridor into the cell block. A flick of Petro's light showed a dozen barred cubicles. On the deck above shouts were rising. Men tripped over each other in alarm, and someone was yelping for battle lanterns. Petro searched the cells in the dim lantern light. "Mauki?"

"Yes, yes!" the woman said in the darkness. "Hurry."

A cutting torch flared, and sparks flew up as the bars yielded to intense heat. Tiny held a tangle-gun in his hand, firing steadily as crewmen began tumbling down the ladder into the brig.

Petro felt the woman's hand in his. "Quickly," she said. "There's another way out to the main corridor. Your torch can cut the lock."

"Where's the child?" Petro asked.

"The child is dead. They jettisoned him without a suit."

A growl rose in Petro's throat. He whistled for Tiny and followed the woman back along the row of cells. As crewmen stumbled and cursed in the darkness, the raiders burst through into the main corridor and through the holds and storage bins toward the exit hatch, with Tiny holding the rear as Petro and the woman plunged ahead. Panic reigned in the quarters below; crewmen were fighting each other as the ship's officers roared helplessly for order. Petro found Jack waiting for them at the exit. The raiders were scrambling across into their own fleet space craft while the Earth crew was still floundering. As he slammed the airlock shut, Petro saw that the woman was still clutching in her arms the empty hood and pressure suit of a five-year-old child.

Moments later, the raider craft shot away from the hull of the Earth ship, sliding back into the blackness behind the asteroid. "All right," Petro said grimly. "Battle stations." The tiny ship turned its six missile tubes to face the Earth ship. "Ready with one and two."

The mauki had been huddled in the corner of the cabin, sobbing. Now she looked up, tears still streaking her face. "What are you going to do?"

"What do you think I'm going to do?" Petro said harshly. "They're butchers. Kidnaping you is one thing. Murdering a five-year-old child is something else. Well, they haven't even got their battle lights on yet. We'll gut them."

The woman was on her feet. "No, please! Let them go back home."

"So they can murder more of our children?"

"You don't understand. They were afraid of him."

"Of a *five-year-old?*"

"Yes, they were afraid—until they heard me sing."

Petro stared at her, hesitating, while Jack and Tiny waited for the order. "Please," the woman said, "let them go home."

Petro shrugged and turned away, striking his fist viciously in his palm. "It's idiocy. We have them helpless."

"And if we killed them, we would be no better than they," the woman said quietly. "Is that what you want? If there is ever to be an end to this war, someone has to rise above it sometime."

Petro and his men stared at one another. Then Petro sighed. "All right," he said. "Close the tubes. Head back to Central, while I try to think of something to tell the Council. And make it fast."

Tiny and Jack set the course. Slowly the ship eased back and away, then lost itself in the blackness of space, moving out toward the heart of the Asteroid Belt. Hours later, with generators repaired and power restored, the hulking Earth ship sneaked out of its hiding place, scanning the area for ambush, and began its long, ponderous orbit back toward Earth.

The Earth ship knew, of course, what the raiders could have done. Every man in the crew knew that, from the captain down, and no one could understand why they had been allowed to escape. Yet in their minds the haunting chant of the captive woman still echoed; they could still hear her song of longing and loneliness. Back on Earth they would remember those words, and talk about that song for years to come.

And that was what the mauki wanted.

1 THE RUMOR

It was not really any great desire to display his skill as a pilot that led Ben Trefon to pancake his little four-seater down for a crazy pinwheel landing on the Martian desert that late afternoon in the spring. He certainly hadn't planned it that way, and the fact that he nearly dumped the little space craft into the Great Rift before he finally got it landed on the red desert sand didn't mean that he was particularly reckless most times. Of course, he didn't know that half the Central Council was watching his landing from his father's front terrace, and it was fairly common knowledge that a Spacer didn't stay alive very long if he wasn't a little reckless once in a while. As far as Ben Trefon was concerned, the near-disaster was mostly his father's fault for recalling him home to Mars so suddenly, without warning or explanation, when he knew that other more exciting things were afoot.

As a matter of fact, at the age of eighteen Ben Trefon was a highly expert space pilot. From his fifth birthday on he had been familiar with the feel of space ship controls. He had handled the whole range of Spacer ships, from the tiniest one-man scooters to the great cargo ships orbiting home from the raids on Earth. He had learned the principles of inertia of motion and inertia of rest almost before he learned his ABC's, and the laws of gravity and null-gravity seemed more natural than addition and subtraction. When he had later come up against the theory of interplanetary navigation, astrophysics, landing maneuvers and raiding techniques at the Spacer Academy on Asteroid Central, he had brought with him a dozen years of experience in practical, seat-of-the-pants space flying.

But things seemed to conspire against Ben Trefon ever since his father's message came through to him on Asteroid Central forty-eight hours before. The forthcoming raid was Ben's first as a full-fledged participant, and the briefings and instructions had gone on all through the night. For days the excitement had been mounting until the whole raiding crew was running on raw nerve and tension . . . and then Dad's message, like a dash of ice-cold water in his face: RETURN TO MARS AT ONCE. URGENT THAT I SEE YOU BEFORE THE RAID. REPEAT, URGENT.

That in itself was unnerving. Dad didn't go in for heavy drama. He knew as well as any Spacer the tension that built up before a major raid on Earth. He would never have sent a summons like that unless something were drastically wrong. That knowledge alone worried Ben all the way home and affected his judgment when he decided to make a powered landing on the Martian desert without the aid of his ship's null-gravity units.

He knew that he had trapped himself the moment he swung the little ship into its first graceful braking arc through the tenuous outer layers of the Martian atmosphere. He could have backed out and used the null-grav units in the next pass but with typical Trefon stubbornness, he decided to bull it through, and that was his *real* mistake. As he watched the surface of the red planet skimming by below him, he realized that he needed one more hand and one more foot than he had to keep his ship under control. He spotted his landing target, the great camouflaged patchwork of the House of Trefon resting on a low plateau near the equator on the edge of the Great Rift, and things looked all right until his third braking arc when the massive north-moving jet stream caught the little ship and carried it fifteen degrees off course. He was still farther off course as the ship swept around over the dark side of Mars; on the next pass the atmosphere was thicker and Ben's attempt to compensate with more and more torque from the ship's side jets made control all the harder.

By the time he came into his final arc for landing, he was riding the little craft like a bucking bronco, trying to prevent a side-slip, with his approach speed twice too fast and the long, deep canyon of the Rift yawning larger and larger ahead of him. The ship rolled crazily as Ben fought the controls; then, in desperation, he slammed on the forward braking jet and said a quick prayer. His body strained at the safety belt as force slammed against force and the tiny ship jerked as if it had struck a stone wall. Then its nose dropped suddenly and the ground rushed up at him. One landing skid struck the edge of the Rift; in graceful slow motion the ship did an end-over-end pirouette in the air and bounced on its belly three times before coming to a stop in a cloud of red desert sand.

Ben sat for a moment or two, gathering his wits and catching his breath as the dust settled. He could see the shiny plastic bubble of his father's house on the dunes above him. Already a crash siren was wailing. An emergency sand-cat rolled down the hill toward him from the house, with a second following in its tracks. By the time Ben climbed out of the cockpit, feeling very foolish, the sand-cats reached him.

He waved to the ground crew and jumped down onto the sand. The plastic lid of the first sand-cat flew up, and Elmo Peterson, his father's chief mechanic, glared down at Ben from the controls. "Crazy kid!" he bellowed. "What were you trying to do, land that thing on its back?"

"The jet stream caught me," Ben said defensively, climbing into the sand-cat.

"Well, what did you expect?" Peterson was a big man, with a shock of snow-white hair like most Spacer men. "You never heard of null-gravity, I suppose? Your dad nearly swallowed his tongue."

"Count on him to be watching," Ben said sourly. "What does he want me for, anyway?"

Peterson ignored the question for a moment as he mustered the ground crew to haul Ben's ship—on its bent landing skids—up to the hangar. Then he turned the sand-cat around on its caterpillar tracks and headed toward the house again. "Right now he may just want to take a belt to you," he answered Ben finally. "He wasn't the only one watching that little performance."

A moment later Ben saw what the big man meant. The House of Trefon, like all Spacer homes built on Mars or the major asteroids, was artfully concealed from detection from above. But as the sand-cat ground up the hill toward the bubble-enclosed buildings, Ben could see that the hangar area was filled with private space craft. A dozen small ships were here, old and new, with the ground crew working frantically to service them. Some of them Ben recognized at once: there was old Mitsuki Mikuta's tiny private ship up against the hangar wall; Dan O'Brien's flambuoyant yellow craft was being polished down by three of the ground crew, and across the hangar he could see Roger Petro's new black-and-white family cruiser.

Ben stared at Peterson. "Is the whole Council here?"

"Pretty near it," Peterson said. "And the rest will be here before long."

"But why? What's going on?"

Peterson shrugged. "Ask your dad. They don't ask *my* permission for a Council meeting."

Ben fought down his rising alarm, but it wouldn't work. "You must have heard something," he pleaded. "This isn't going to stall the raid, is it? I mean, they aren't going to call it off for some reason?"

Peterson hauled the sand-cat in through the airlock of the plastic bubble, and snapped the motor off. "Look," he said patiently. "Just ask your dad, huh? I've got a hunch he's looking for you."

"I suppose," Ben said gloomily, climbing down to the hangar floor. "Well, thanks for the lift."

"Anytime," Peterson said. "And Ben, if you need some liniment for your backside later on, I think I can find some in the shop."

Ben grinned and started up the ramp that led into the house. Strong and silent, that was Elmo Peterson. But this time, somehow, Elmo's silence had an ominous ring to it. It was no accident that the Spacer Council was convening on the eve of a major Earth raid. Ben Trefon was certain of that. And if he had suspected trouble when his father's summons came, he was sure of it now.

The House of Trefon on Mars was not large, as Spacer houses go. You could find a dozen larger houses scattered here and there across the surface of Mars, or on Juno or Ceres, on Ganymede and Europa of Jupiter, or even on Titan and Japetus of Saturn, if you knew where to look for them. Probably no more than a dozen Spacer families were ever living in the House of Trefon at any one time . . . and yet this house, like all large Spacer houses, was a buzzing community in itself, with its own warehouses and storerooms, its own schools, its own laboratories and its own fabricating plants. And like other Spacer dwellings, Ben Trefon thought, it had an uncanny air of impermanence about it, as though it had been thrown together willy-nilly, a piece at a time, and might suddenly vanish again overnight in just as haphazard a fashion as it was built.

Partly, of course, the architecture of the place led to this feeling: the tall, spidery arches, the vast expanses of the dome-ceilinged rooms, the shimmering movement of the plastic sheet walls. Spacers had enough of tight quarters and enclosed spaces in their ships; in their houses they wanted space, and freedom and long vistas. But even more important, the houses reflected the people who lived in them. No Spacer, once he was out of his childhood classrooms, ever seemed to stay in one place very long at a time. Spacers laughed with open scorn at the crowded, hive-like cities of the Earthbound people, and really felt completely at home only in the cabins of their roving ships, moving at will through the length and breadth of the solar system, through the familiar blackness and the sweeping distances of interplanetary space.

Yet Ben Trefon now felt a surge of pleasure and contentment as he walked up the ramp and into the great receiving hall of his father's house. He sniffed at the familiar tinge of ozone in the artificial atmosphere and listened to the soft, solid thump of his feet on the red sandstone flagstones as he crossed through to the private wings of the house. He was a small, wiry youth with a spring in his step and the first hint of premature gray in his hair. With the rich oxygen ratio in the house his cheeks were pinker than usual, and he felt the usual exhilaration in spite of the worry that was nagging at his mind.

He crossed the concourse leading to the community center and common rooms. Once inside his family's private quarters, he checked the call board and saw that only half a dozen families were checked in. He realized then what it was he had missed as he came in through the entry hall. There had been no sign of the crowd of small boys who were usually running and shouting, chasing each other to be first to greet him on other occasions when he had returned to the House of Trefon.

Ben scratched his head, flipped on the daylight screens, and dropped his space pack on a canvas armchair as late afternoon light filled the room. This was a combination study and living room, with books and tapes piled in disorderly array against the plastic walls; farther back were the sun deck and the sleeping quarters, the only part of the private quarters that Dad ever managed to keep as neat and sparkling as when Mom was alive. Ben drifted from room to room, eager to see his father, wondering, as he had wondered so often before, if things would have been different for them all if his mother had lived long enough for him to know her. Not that he didn't get along with Dad; they were friends, and they respected each other. But always there were Spacer affairs to be taken care of, reports to prepare for the Council, plans to be made, and never somehow quite enough time for father and son to get to know each other well.

Ben Trefon felt his father's presence in the room before he heard him. Ivan Trefon might have been a carbon copy of his son, except for the added years that showed in the lines of his face and the whiteness of his hair. He took off his glasses and stared at his son for a long moment, then touched his forehead in a mock salute. "So the astronaut returns," he said wryly. "Welcome home. For a minute there I thought old Dusty Red had you for sure."

Ben flushed at the old Spacer nickname for Mars, and at the gentle warning his father was implying. He knew as well as any Spacer the terrible toll of lives old Dusty Red had taken before ships had been equipped with null-gravity units. "I misjudged it," Ben said. "I should never have tried landing without null-grav."

Ivan Trefon chuckled. "You don't look very penitent, somehow. Just be glad a license inspector wasn't watching you land. You'd have gone back to the practice ships for the next five years." The older man regarded his son quizzically. "Though I have to give you credit. Once you'd trapped yourself, you pulled it off pretty well. I'd have gone into the Rift for sure."

"They teach us to fly ships these days, not just pull levers," Ben replied. "And that was one of the new S-80's, too. Have you ever flown one? They make the old four-seaters look like cargo ships, handle so smoothly you hardly know you're out there." He hesitated, trying to read his father's face. "I should have been checking in at the rendezvous with that ship right now, dad. As it is, I'll miss the final briefing. Why did you want me here?"

Ivan Trefon looked suddenly older, and very tired. "Maybe just an old man's whim. Wanted a look at my boy before he left on his first raid."

"And the Council meeting?" Ben said. "Is *that* an old man's whim? You aren't that old, dad. What's gone wrong? Something surely has. And it's got something to do with the raid. What is it?"

The older man turned away and shrugged his shoulders. "It's very simple," he said quietly. "I want to stop this raid. I've been trying ever since it was planned. I've spent the last three days trying to get the Council to put the brakes on it, and so far I haven't won. It's beginning to look as if I'm not going to, either." He looked across at Ben. "So there you have it."

Ben's eyes reflected his astonishment. "Stop the raid? But I don't understand. Why?"

"Because it has to be stopped."

"That's no answer, and you know it."

Ivan Trefon smiled ruefully. "So the Council has been telling me. If I had a better answer, maybe they'd listen." He stopped smiling and looked at Ben. "This is your first raid, isn't it?"

"The first real one. I've been down twice with a scouting party, and once on a mock raid, but never the real thing before."

"What do you know about this raid? What's your objective? What are you striking for?"

"Food," Ben Trefon said. "Wheat, beef, staples . . . supplies are getting low, and we can't live on Martian barley."

"Where's the strike point?"

"North American mid-continent. There's a central food warehouse there with over a thousand wheat storage bins. Our contact men already have them rigged with null-grav units. All we need is an orbit ship to scoop them in, and a crew to go down and activate the units."

"And fight off the guard units stationed in the warehouse," Ivan Trefon said.

"Even that's been taken care of," Ben said eagerly. "The word has been leaked out that our strike point will be a South American food dump. And they've garrisoned that one to the teeth and pulled most of the guard strength away from the real objective."

"And what about women?" the older man said.

"Well, there's that on any raid, naturally," Ben said. "But the last raid filled the quota pretty well, so only the first-timers are expected to bring back girls this time." He shrugged disgustedly. "Matter of fact, that's *all* my personal orders will let me do on this raid . . . find a good mauki prospect and haul her back here. But you already know all this. The Council has the whole plan from the Raid Commander. Why are you asking me?"

"To see if you know what you're walking into," Ivan Trefon said.

"Well, there's nothing very exciting about kidnaping a girl," Ben admitted. "But on the next raid they'll let me do more."

His father nodded slowly. "If there is a next raid."

Suddenly Ben could feel the tension in the air, the strain and tiredness in his father's voice. "Dad, what are you talking about? What's wrong? Why did you call me down here?"

"Because I don't want you to go on this raid."

"You mean you want me to scratch?"

"That's right. I want you to scratch."

Ben was silent for a moment, staring at his father. Then

he sighed. "Dad, look. I know that the raids are dangerous. But I've been training for weeks. I can take care of myself."

The older man shook his head impatiently. "It's not that. If I let myself worry about you taking care of yourself, I'd have cracked up years ago."

"Then what is it? What's wrong?"

Ivan Trefon walked across the room to the light screen, and stared out at the darkening Martian desert. The sun was almost at the horizon now, bathing the rolling sand hills in deep purple light. Already the sky above was black, and the stars were showing by the hundreds. The old man turned and looked at his son squarely. "I don't know what's wrong, not for sure," he said. "If I did, I swear that I'd tell you. All I know for sure is that *something* is wrong. Something is going on, down on Earth, that our best intelligence men there can't crack. The Earthmen have it under security wraps so tight that we can't even get a toe in the door. All we can get is rumors, but the rumors sound bad."

"Rumors about what?"

"About a blow-out," Ivan Trefon said. "Not just another of their silly reprisals. Not just a vigilante ship coming out to kidnap and torture a mauki or two. I mean a real blow-out."

"But what *else* could they do?" Ben asked incredulously. "They can't mount a fleet against us . . . anybody knows that."

"I'm not so sure," his father said slowly. "How much do you know about what's been going on?"

"You mean between Earthmen and Spacers?"

"That's right."

Ben scratched his jaw. "Well . . . I know what everybody else knows."

"Like what, for instance?"

"That Earth is theirs and space is ours. That they slammed the door on us centuries ago, and that we've never been able to break it open again. And that sometime we'll grow strong enough to force the door open so that we won't have to raid them any more for food and women and other things we need. Then we can come and go as we please on Earth and they can come and go as they please in space."

Ivan Trefon shook his head grimly. "It's a pretty dream, I know," he said. "Even I used to believe it, a long time ago."

"You mean you think that we'll never have peace?" Ben said.

"I'm afraid that's what I mean."

"But why not?"

"Because they hate us," Ivan Trefon said. "They hate us and they fear us. They fear the slightest contact with us, as if we had some kind of horrible disease. I never really realized how much they hated us until we had the meeting last year with their emissaries."

Ben stared. "You—you had a *meeting* with them?"

The older man nodded. "The Council never released the news. It was a pretty ugly meeting, and we learned later that they executed their own emissaries in space on their way home after their reports were taped. They were afraid even to let them set foot back on Earth. But we learned a lot from that meeting."

"Like what?"

"A few simple facts that we'd known for a long time, but never really believed," Ivan Trefon said wearily. "We learned that Earth will never settle for peace with us. They won't even settle for enslaving us. They want us dead. Every man, every woman, every child of us—dead. Those were their terms for peace. And now our contact men down there are worried. Money has been going somewhere, and they can't find out where. In the past five years more and more of Earth's total labor force has been working on something that hasn't appeared on the public market. The standard of living has dropped over fifty per cent, farms are lying idle, factories have closed down. Everything has been changing in the last five years, and now it's beginning to look as if something is ready to break loose."

Ben Trefon was silent for a long moment. Then he shook his head. "And you think that whatever they're doing is somehow tied into this raid?"

"I think something is ready to break. I think this raid could be the trigger to set it off."

"But don't you see that this is all the more reason why I can't back out?" Ben said. "Dad, we can't survive without the raids. Sooner or later somebody is going to have to go down there. And I've been tapped for this raiding party. I can't stay home just because you're afraid something terrible is going to happen."

His father looked up at him. "'You're determined to go, then."

"Of course I'm determined to go. But I'm worried about you, now. You sound—" Ben groped for words.

"Like I'm losing my grip?" Ivan Trefon laughed. "Like a frightened old man, trying to scare you away with spooks?"

"Well, maybe not," Ben said soberly. "But you're frightened, whether you know it or not. And there's nothing to be frightened of. We've been raiding Earth for centuries. Nothing different is going to happen this time than any other time." Ben shrugged. "So maybe they have some fancy plan for beating us off. What do we care? The only thing they could possibly do to hurt us would be to mount a fleet against us, a space fleet. And everybody knows they can't do that. They don't know how, and they're afraid to try."

"I suppose," Ivan Trefon said sadly. "Well, if you're determined, nothing I can say is going to stop you. But you can't say I didn't try. Good luck, boy. And good hunting."

Ben clasped his father's hand. "I'll need both, if I'm going to bring back a mauki. You might buzz Elmo in the shop and tell him I won't need that liniment, after all." He turned and started for the door, his mind still filled with uneasiness. What was it that was bothering Dad? What was it he was trying to say, and still had left unsaid? At the door he turned back, searching his father's tired face. "Was there anything else, before I go?"

Ivan Trefon shook his head slowly. "No, not really. Not now. But Ben—" He hesitated. "You know where the vaults are?"

"You mean down below?"

The old man nodded. "The lock was keyed to your handprint the day you were born. There are certain things which require attention there, after I'm gone. When the time comes, I must count on you to open the vault. You will be responsible for what you find there."

"When the time comes?"

"If anything should happen to me."

"Of course. You can count on it."

His father took a deep breath. "Good," he said. "Now you'd better move, before the night winds give you a rough takeoff."

Moments later Ben Trefon was walking back through the deserted entry hall toward the ramp to the hangar. Lights were coming on now, but there was still an eerie silence about the place, as though some portion of the life had somehow gone out of the House of Trefon. Ben frowned as he started down the ramp, still puzzling over his father's last words. Down in the hangar his little S-80 was waiting, fully fuelled, the bent landing skid straightened and welded. His mind turned back to the excitement of the forthcoming raid. He checked out for launching, climbed into the cabin and waited as the winches drew the little ship out through the airlock and placed it on the long launching track.

And then, with a roar of power and the whine of antigravity engines reverberating in his ears, Ben Trefon lifted the little ship swiftly into the dark sky and watched the House of Trefon dwindle to a speck on the Martian desert below him. Maybe when he came back, he thought, his father would explain what it was that he still had left unsaid. But somehow Ben knew, even now, that he was leaving behind in this house something he would never regain. He shifted the controls gently, and watched as the ship moved out from behind the disc of Mars and headed like a tiny arrow in toward the orbit of Earth.

2 THE RAID

SOMEWHERE FAR below the dark side of the planet Earth glowed dimly up in the ashen light from the moon. Hardly breathing, Ben Trefon watched the great gray disc loom steadily larger in the view screen of his scout ship. For the hundredth time he checked the approach pattern of lights on the control panel before him; each tiny fleck of light represented one of his companion ships. He adjusted the controls, felt the little ship veer slightly as he brought it back into proper alignment with the others. There was no sign of the other ships in his view screen. The flat-black paint on their hulls reflected no light, and the ships were darkened, moving toward their target like shadows out of the blackness of space.

From the perimeter of the dark planet below a tiny fleck of light appeared, turning in a slow curve, then blinking out again as it moved into Earth's shadow. It was an early warning satellite, moving in a low, watchful orbit around Earth. Ben smiled grimly to himself. That would mean that Earth now knew the raiders were coming. Long since, the great radar screens on the planet's surface must have picked out the pattern of the raiding ships: over three hundred reflecting fragments of metal, moving in close formation straight down toward the planet's surface from their rendezvous with the orbit ship hiding behind the moon. The Earthmen knew the raid was coming, all right, and Ben could imagine the furious preparations going on below to greet the raiders at the expected target site.

But now the time for patience and planning was over. From this point on speed, striking power, certainty of purpose and skill were the raiders' weapons as they converged like a swarm of bees on a target too late discovered to be properly protected. Each of the raiding ships, each of the men now piloting a ship through Earth's atmosphere and gravitational field had his own individual assignment. The raid had been rehearsed; the advance planning had been perfected, reviewed, revised and re-perfected. It was this planning that had always, invariably, made the raids on Earth so successful. The Spacers had no equals when it came to navigational skill. They had learned through the centuries to strike hard and fast, to get their work done and to get out, always leaving behind them a wave of confusion and terror.

Such raids were dangerous, of course, but Ben Trefon had had no time to consider the possible dangers. He never gave thought to the fact that he might not leave the surface of this planet alive. As always, the goal of the raid was simple and explicit: five million tons of wheat stored in the granaries south of the metropolis called Chicago in the center of the northern hemisphere continent; fifteen thousand tons of dressed beef stored in the vast cold storage lockers of the packing plants a little farther north in the great city; and last but not least, thirty women, not younger than fifteen years, not older than twenty-five, to fulfill the quota required by the Spacer Council at the time of its last census.

Already the groundwork for the raid was finished. Spies on the planet's surface, their hair dyed to conceal the telltale whiteness, had worked for many nights excavating the grain storage units at target site and placing the antigravity rods beneath them, so that the raiders had only to connect the rods to their ships' generators to raise the bins up through Earth's atmosphere to a place where each orbit ship could scoop them into its hold. A quick landing of a few dozen ships in the right places was all it would take; fifteen minutes of swift work by the ships' crews, while a covering crew fought rear-guard action with any defending troops that arrived in time, a few swift moves, and the Spacers would have replenished their dwindling supplies of staple foods once again.

The maukis were a different matter. There it was a matter of swift movement, resourcefulness and imagination on the part of the raiders assigned to kidnap them. Each of the thirty ships assigned was responsible for one woman, and each pilot was responsible for his own escape with his booty. Even though it was seldom discussed, every man in the raiding party knew instinctively that these women were really the most critical prize of all, as far as ultimate survival of the Spacer culture was concerned.

Like all the others, this raid was to follow a rigid pattern. Preparations had been made months in advance: first the drawings to select the crew of the raiding ships; then the assignment of jobs and the selection of squad leaders; then the weeks of drilling and planning, with each anticipated move carefully co-ordinated with all the rest; the checking and double checking with the Spacer contact men stationed on Earth to prepare the ground. There were the mock raids on any one of a dozen specially prepared asteroids in the vicinity of Asteroid Central, and the intensive training of all the men who would pilot ships, to be sure they were fresh in their knowledge of Earth meteorology, atmospheric conditions, geography and the latest figures on defense entrenchments.

It was not unusual for a raid to be six or eight months in preparation. This particular raid had taken five months of intensive hard work before the Raid Commander was satisfied. At last the orbit ship, one of the great spherical interplanetary cargo ships of the Spacer fleet, was commissioned for the raid and thrown into orbit toward the sun. And once again, as in so many raids before, the orbit ship and all the rest of the raiding fleet, from the tiny S-80's to the twenty-man cruisers that handled the big null-gravity generators, began to take their places in a wide orbit around Earth, using the hidden side of Earth's moon for a rendezvous point before the raid began.

In the final gathering at rendezvous the ships maintained strict radio and radar silence, converging on the orbit ship for their last briefing. Up to that point the raid could be cancelled at any moment, either on order from the Spacer Council or on advice of the contact men on Earth. But once zero hour had arrived and the ships had begun their final drive down to the surface of the planet, there was no stopping. The raiders knew that from that point on they were on their own, that the success or failure of the raid was in their hands.

Ben Trefon had seen many pictures of the verdant planet that lay in his view screen now. He had seen picture tapes of the rolling farm lands, carefully operated to provide the biggest possible food yields for the teeming millions of people living there. He had seen films of the huge steel caves, the great tiered cities that spread over the largest part of the planet's surface, the hive-like homes of the Earthmen. He had seen pictures of the rolling roads that criss-crossed the planet to carry food and supplies from continent to continent, and of the undersea farms that grew algae and sea food, the staples of the Earthmen's diet. From time to time he knew that Spacer raids had struck at the huge floating harvest rafts, many square miles across, which floated on the major oceans of the planet and tended the undersea crops.

But try as he would, as he watched the planet approaching, Ben Trefon could not imagine what life on a planet such as

Earth could be like. Earthmen were planet-bound; not only were their skills in space crude and feeble, they were bound by a fear of space as real as it was incredible to the Spacers. More than once Ben had tried to imagine what it would be like to have been born in one of the steel cities on Earth, to grow up in the underground nurseries and recreation halls, rarely seeing the brightness of the sun at the surface, or breathing the unprocessed air outside, living from birth until death bound to the surface of a single planet without a breath of hope of ever leaving it. More than once he had tried to imagine how Earthmen must feel, living in constant terror of invasion from the skies, with every movement of their lives dictated by a rigid martial law that barely left them freedom to breathe.

But try as he would, he could not imagine it. Of course, he had never actually set foot on Earth before. He had never actually seen an Earthman, and he certainly had never talked to one. But he knew about them, he thought. He knew a good deal indeed. He had heard of their cruelty and viciousness, he knew of their world of cold steel and humming machines, of the clatter of firearms and the test-firing of their great anti-aircraft batteries. He knew of the Earthmen's fear of space, even though he had never been able to understand it, and he had heard of the cruel retaliatory raids and disciplinary parties Earth had sent out into space from time to time in an effort to beat back the harassment of the Spacers. He had heard that the greatest bravery, the ultimate courage that an Earthman could exhibit was to shoot down a Spacer during a raid. He had heard other stories, too, stories that were hard to believe of civilized people, yet stories which fitted into the rest of the picture of Earthmen in his mind: stories of Spacers captured alive during raids, imprisoned in steel cages and hauled through the corridors and passageways of Earth's cities like animals before they were finally burned in public executions.

There had always been such stories, and the war between Earthmen and the men of space had dragged on as long as he could remember, with endless series of blows and counter-blows, endless successions of casualty lists following the raids, and the mournful singing of the maukis in memory of the men who never came back. Every Spacer knew that attempts had been made repeatedly to make peace with the men of Earth, to do away with the raids and to permit peaceful commerce and intercommunication between those who lived beyond the atmosphere of the mother planet and those who lived on the surface. Yet every attempt had failed, and the war continued.

Static burst from the radio at his elbow, and Ben awoke from his thoughts. The planet nearly filled his view screen now, growing larger by the minute, and the raider ships were falling into an orbital pattern as the Raid Commander in the flagship broke radio silence. "All right, men," his voice came through sharply. "They're aware of us now. All hands stand by your tracer rockets. They'll throw up a barrage as soon as they have us tracked. Now stand by for a final checkout."

Ben corrected his controls for drift in the squadron formation and turned his ear to the loudspeaker as the commander began running down the list of squads for the final make-ready check.

"Cruiser squadrons, stand ready. Number one sound off."

"First squad ready, sir."

"Duties?"

"Antigravity generators are fully functional, sir. We are warming up the gyros."

"Then check those couplings again. You won't have time to fiddle with them when we reach the strike point. Next?"

"Second squad ready, sir."

Ben listened as the fleet of ships sounded off in turn. They were entering a braking pattern now, nosing down into the thicker layers of the planet's atmosphere. One by one the squad leaders answered muster, making no attempt at secrecy now. Ben heard his own squad leader, commanding about thirty ships, sound off in response to the muster.

"Seventh squad ready, sir."

"Do your men have their target in mind?"

"Yes, sir. Top level recreation hall near the south city margin. Five red flares to guide us in."

"Then good hunting," the commander said. "And remember: no more violence than necessary. Use your tangle-guns. Those girls aren't maukis yet. Don't make it tough on the indoctrination crews."

Suddenly, down below, four flares of light appeared against the black disk of the planet, and a warning signal began to buzz on Ben's control panel. The commander's checkout was interrupted by a burst of static as another voice broke in sharply. "Now hear this, all ships! Stand by for missile barrage. Ready your homing shells. Those are big ones, and they'll have warheads."

The flares on the surface of the planet seemed to grow larger, moving in a curving trajectory up toward the orbit of the Spacer ships. Then, one by one, the main boosters of the ground-to-air missiles burned out and the smaller guidance jets were flaring on and off as the missiles' sensitive "noses" began searching out their targets in the onrushing fleet. Ben gripped his crash bar tightly, watching for some sign of Spacer counterfire. The missile flares were lost from view behind him now, but he knew they were still coming, moving up swiftly toward the carefully pre-calculated interception point, each carrying a cargo of death for any invading ship it contacted. There was another salvo of the great missiles from below, and then another, and still Ben watched and waited for the Spacer cruisers' answering fire.

And then it came: a dozen sparks of light appearing in the blackness around him as the dark Spacer ships let go their defensive barrage. A swarm of interceptor missiles carrying tracers zoomed down in a great arc toward the oncoming warheads. In his rear view screen Ben watched the silent panorama of red lights moving against the blackness. The Spacer barrage was late; already the warheads were within pickup distance of the lead ships. And if a warhead missile got close enough to enter the invading fleet's approach pattern. . . .

Somewhere below there was a violent flare of yellow light, and then another. Two great fireballs appeared like apparitions in the blackness as Spacer rockets at last reached the attacking missiles and detonated their hydrogen warheads harmlessly in space. Moments later came a third burst below them, too close for comfort, and a few seconds before interception point the fourth exploded. Against the enormous orange flash Ben could see the Spacer ships silhouetted as they moved relentlessly down into their landing orbit.

Safe from the first four! But this was only the beginning. Missile flares were visible across the whole surface of the planet now, and on a sharp command five of the Spacer cruisers dropped out of formation, moving down to a rear-guard position twenty miles below and fifty miles behind the rest of the fleet. Every Spacer ship carried a variety of defensive and offensive missiles, both air-to-air and air-to-ground, but the cruisers were the defensive work horses of the Spacer fleet, prepared to stand off the most vicious ground-to-air attacks. Now Ben could see salvo after salvo of air-to-air missiles bursting from the bellies of the cruisers and zooming down to intercept the clumsy Earth weapons. Fleetingly, Ben thought of his father's warning about some new defense plan the Earthmen had, and he smiled to himself. There was nothing new about this. The same slow, awkward missiles, the same laborious attempts at interception that the Earthmen always tried, with equipment so far outclassed by the swift, sensitive Spacer defensive weapons that it was almost laughable. Not quite laughable, because a few always got through, and a few Spacer ships always exploded in blazing flares of orange light, before the fleet got down below the tactical range of the great missiles. Even so, the defensive attempt was feeble and essentially fruitless, and that was fine, Ben thought. If they want to throw away their hardware this way, that's up to them.

Throughout the barrage, orders came for tactical maneuvering as the Raid Commander led his fleet deftly downward. Below a certain level they would be safe from the hydrogen warheads. As Ben moved his own controls to conform to the changing attack pattern, he saw a mighty flare up ahead—one of the lead Spacer ships was struck. The Earth missile hurled its tons of explosive violence into the very spearhead of the Spacer approach pattern, closely followed by a second. "All right, men," the commander's voice said. "They've spotted our pattern. Now take battle formation. Drop down and rejoin over the strike point."

Ben threw his control levers forward, veering his ship out of the vortex of destruction up ahead, and nosing it down deeper into the thickening atmospheric blanket of the planet. The little ship's skin temperature began to rise, and he navigated on his own, trying to gauge his speed by the approach to critical skin temp. Speed and agility were essential now, but unwary ships had literally burned themselves to cinders by trying to move down too swiftly. This was the danger area, the missile belt where every Spacer ship had to rely on its own protective devices. In order to make as poor targets as possible, it was routine for raiding fleets to spread themselves over millions of square miles, each pilot taking a course with but one goal in mind: to drop down to the surface, decelerate as swiftly as atmospheric friction would allow, and somehow stay alive in the process.

For all the great distances to be covered, the Spacer ships were coming in fast. The dark planet's surface gave way to a twilight zone, and then full daylight as they moved around into the sun. Ben could see the fleecy white cloud layers clinging to the planet's skin like a great fur coat. There was a rift in the clouds, and the shattering glare of water reflecting the sun struck his eyes. He was over ocean now. Moments later he was skimming into thicker atmosphere, one hand on radio control as he sent out feelers to locate the other ships in his squad.

One responded; then another. Presently he could see the other ships, moving in with him to gather for their landing pattern, and the squad leader was calling signals. Now they were back across twilight to the dark side of Earth; the clouds opened up and they could see below them the pattern of surface lights outlining first the coastal cities of the western hemisphere northern continent, and then the vast blanket of light from the interior metropolis they were seeking, extending north and south for three hundred miles and east and west for two hundred: the city of Chicago with its seventy million people and the food storage warehouses designed to keep them fed.

Ben smiled in satisfaction. They had moved in so fast that blackout had not even yet been accomplished. A slower operation and they would have had to search their way with flares and follow directional signals from their contact men below. Now Ben was following the signals of his squad leader almost automatically, obeying landing instructions as the anti-aircraft flack burst on all sides of him. One of his companion ships was struck and burst apart in air, but Ben did not falter at the controls. He worked his null-gravity controls now, leading the ship down in a descending spiral. Somewhere below bright red ground flares appeared in a pattern of a five-pointed star; moments later, with his null-grav engines whining Ben set his little ship slowly down in the center of the area marked by the flares, felt the ship jar as it gently settled to a stop.

He was on target zero.

Whatever Ben Trefon had expected to see when he landed his S-80 at the strike point designated for him, he was unprepared for the nightmarish scene that greeted him as he checked the tangle-gun at his belt and threw open the lock to step down on the surface of the planet Earth for the first time.

Their approach had been so swift, and the landing flares set off so shortly before their ships touched down that blackout in the target area had been incomplete and, on the concourse outside, the raiding ships were faced by a panic-stricken and hysterical mob. Ben's ship had settled down on a broad steel thoroughfare lined with shops and gardens, with a great brightly lighted hall just across the strip from his ship. A dozen other S-80's had landed in the vicinity, all but encircling the hall, and as Ben stepped down on the metal surface of the concourse, the frantic scurrying of people, obviously interrupted without warning in the midst of their evening business on the concourse, reminded him of a pack of space mice scurrying for cover in a cargo ship's hold when the lights suddenly went on. Sirens were screaming in his ears as he jumped down, signalling his companions from the other ships, and somewhere in the distance he heard a rattle of gun-fire and a series of explosions that seemed to shake the metal roadway.

They had landed on a promenade, located at the surface level of the great steel Earth city, a metal strip that seemed to extend for miles in either direction, with open air shops, restaurants, recreation halls and solariums. Ben knew something of the ways of city life on this crowded planet; he knew that these surface promenades in the open air were largely the domain of the wealthy and influential on Earth, for there simply was not enough surface room on the planet to allow all members of society to have free access to the top levels of the city areas. Even so, the promenades were usually crowded with pleasure seekers in the evenings, and it was only the arrival of unexpected company that had created the pandemonium that greeted his eyes now.

People were fighting and screaming to gain entrance to the buildings, to get under cover somehow from the attackers. Lights along the promenade were going out in rapid succession, and surface cars were scurrying up and down the thoroughfare and ducking off into secondary alleys like frightened beetles scurrying under rocks. Inside the recreation hall nearest to Ben's ship there were shrieks and shouts as someone bellowed at the top of his lungs for order. Crowds of young people, who had been enjoying the freedom of the open air just a few moments before, were now rushing for the escalators and elevators leading down into the heart of the city, and people were trampling and fighting their way toward light switches in an effort to black out the hall and surrounding area.

Ben snapped on the powerful searchlights on his S-80, flooding the entrance to the recreation hall with light. Two other raider craft had landed close to him: now searchlight beams appeared on the far side of the hall, and Ben knew that Spacer ships had encircled the place in landing. The pilot of the nearest ship waved at Ben, tangle-gun in hand, and ran across to meet him, panting.

"Let's get in there and stop those elevators," he cried. "They're going down the escalators like rats down a chute!"

"Where are the others?" Ben said.

"Coming in from the other side. But we'd better move. The place will be empty in a few minutes."

Ben nodded, and they moved toward the recreation hall entrance as two other raiders joined them. Ben held his tangle-gun at ready, fingering the grenades at his belt with the other hand. Two young men with terror-filled faces were blocking the entrance, unarmed, and Ben and his cohorts bore down on them. Ben caught the first man a full body block, shoving him aside with sheer momentum; the Spacers behind him followed close as he crashed through the entranceway. Once inside the raiders scattered to take up pre-planned stations about the room.

The escalators were their first concern. Already they were carrying loads of people down, a tangle of struggling arms and legs, but moving down inexorably. As they saw the Spacers crowd through the entranceway, some dove headfirst down the escalator chutes. Ben threatened the crowd at the escalator entrance with his tangle-gun, motioning them back until the moving staircase had carried its load down and stood empty. Then he tossed a grenade down the chute, and the escalator gears ground to a halt. There was another explosion as a grenade smashed the elevator doors and another as the cables were wrecked. In less than two minutes the hall was sealed up, with no exit unguarded. Two large men rushed Ben with angry shouts; he waited coolly until they were close enough, then triggered the tangle-gun, aiming at their feet. The egg-shaped gray pellet smashed on the floor beneath them, sending up twisting black tendrils of tangle web that stopped them as though they had been poleaxed. Both tumbled to the floor, struggling against the powerful adhesive of the tangle web, bound tighter and tighter as its molecular structure tightened the more they fought to extricate themselves. Nobody ever died from an encounter with a tangle web, but anybody caught in one would be held for hours in its tenacious tendrils, able to breath but not much more, until the molecular activation gradually seeped away and allowed the victim to release himself.

For the first time, Ben had a moment to look around. He was in a hall such as he had never seen before. One of the walls was lined with crowded bookshelves; there were chairs and tables scattered around for lounging, and against the far wall was a big stone box set into the wall with a roaring fire of wood—precious wood!—burning inside. In another large room off to the right were handball courts and a basketball floor, and off to the left—Ben stopped and peered in amazement, hardly believing his eyes. He was looking into another room, with a huge tank of water sunk into the floor. Even now people in skin-tight clothes were struggling to get out of the water and up onto the dry floor. At first Ben thought that the tank was occupied only by men. Suddenly, he realized that some were wearing tight rubber caps and decidedly were not men.

He shouted to his companions:

"Here we go, boys! Over here!"

A dozen Spacers were now in the hall, guarding the exits with tangle-guns. Half a dozen joined him at the entrance to the pool, and began roaring with laughter at the wet, dripping Earth people crowding against the wall. "All right," Ben said sharply. "You men peel off to the right here. No funny business and nobody will be hurt."

The men stood frozen, looking first at the girls huddled at the side of the pool, then at the advancing Spacers. "Come on, *move!*" Ben said. Reluctantly the men began to move.

Ben and two others crossed the room while the rest of the Spacers covered them from the doorway. The girls crowded back against the wall. Some were sobbing; others just looked angry or indignant.

"Volunteers first," Ben said.

Nobody budged. In the main hall a renewed clamor was arising, and Ben heard a rattle of gunfire from somewhere outside. "Come on, we can't wait all night." He motioned the first girl with his tangle-gun. "You, now. Get moving."

"Moving where?" the girl snapped angrily.

"Out of here," Ben said. "You're going for a ride."

"You can't do this," the girl returned. "You can't just walk in and kidnap—"

"Ma'am, you'd be surprised," Ben said. "You can argue later. Right now you can either walk out or be carried out. Which is it to be?"

Furious, the girl stalked past him. Another followed as he motioned to her, and another. At the same moment three of the Earthmen rushed one of the guards. All three were stopped by tangle webs, and one, struggling helplessly, tumbled headfirst into the pool.

"Haul him out," Ben shouted to the guard. "The idiot will drown. But the next one that interferes gets tossed in."

By now almost a dozen girls had been taken into custody

by waiting Spacers, and they started across the main hall toward the door. Now the Earthmen, goaded to ill judgment, tried to move in in a body; tangle-guns popped, and the men shouted and strained at the sticky webs. Ben's gun recoiled in his hand as he placed a shell under the feet of an onrushing man; the attacker twisted to get free of the entangling strands and tumbled to the floor, roaring with anger and shaking his fist at Ben in helpless rage.

But Ben was busy helping his companions single out the girls who gave some outward appearance of spirit and fight. There was no way to guess from a casual glance what kind of mauki a girl might become, but experience had proven that the cringing ones would be more burden than blessing in the long days of re-education and indoctrination that lay ahead of them. In a few moments the full quota of girls was filled except for one; Ben's eye caught a small, attractive girl who had been edging through the group toward the far side of the room.

Ben pointed a finger at her. "You," he said. "Come along."

The girl's bathing cap had come off, revealing a crop of sandy-colored hair. There were large freckles across her nose and cheeks, and a dangerous light in her blue eyes as she stopped and turned toward Ben.

"You don't want me," she said. "I'm pretty ugly." As if to demonstrate her undesirability, she looked cross-eyed and stuck her tongue out at him in a horrible grimace.

Ben grinned. "You'll do," he said. "Come on, hop!"

"But I like it here." The girl was waving her hands frantically, as if trying to signal. Ben thought for a moment he glimpsed a light-haired youth flip his hand in an answering signal.

The hubbub outside was increasing. One of the guards at the door shouted at Ben. "Let's go, boy. We've got a goon squad coming up on us outside."

"All right," Ben said to the sandy-haired girl. "Move on, or I'll carry you."

The girl gave him a long, angry look and, then started past him toward the door. As she came near she jumped at him, quick as a cat, brushing his tangle-gun aside with one hand and hitting him full in the chest with her knees. Ben crashed to the floor, the girl still on his chest, kicking with one foot at the hand that held the tangle-gun. Fighting off nails and teeth, Ben twisted his body out from under the girl, jerking her ankle and toppling her over on her back. She kicked him in the shin, and jumped to her feet again with a cry, once more rushing him. But this time he was ready. He stepped aside swiftly, shooting out his leg to trip her. Seconds later a tangle-gun charge popped on the floor, and the girl was busy trying to fight off the twisting adhesive strands that wrapped around her arms and legs. Without ceremony Ben took one arm and the opposite leg, hoisted her to his shoulders like a sack of meal, and headed for the door at a dead run.

In the main hall there was a confusion of noise and moving figures, and out on the promenade there was gunfire. Some of the searchlights had already gone out on the waiting ships, and Ben found himself tripping over people in the dim light. Then a giant flare burst outside the recreation hall, and a dozen Earthmen, gathering their wits, started converging on him and his wriggling burden. He still gripped his tangle-gun, and cleared a path, but people were grabbing at his arms and legs as he twisted across the room. Two men blocked his way at the door; he headed straight for them, saw one of them dive for his legs, deftly side-stepped and shoved the man's hulk into the path of the other as he burst out onto the promenade.

Once outside, he paused to make sense out of the confusion. A squad of Earth police had arrived and were trying to deploy themselves to prevent the Spacers from regaining their ships, but with the girls as hostages the raiders were safe from gunfire. A shout went up from the onlookers as Ben came out the door, and three uniformed men headed in his direction. Somebody shouted, "There he goes! Get him!" And then, "Hold it—he's got a girl!"

Across the way there was a mighty explosion, and the Spacer ship next to Ben's blossomed into a ball of yellow flame. Some of his companions were making dashes for their ships with girls on their shoulders; two had already been relieved of their booty and were struggling in the arms of police. Ben heard the whine of bullets as they ricocheted off the metal promenade.

For a moment it looked hopeless. Then Ben heard the whir of antigravity generators, and one of the raiding ships lifted suddenly from the ground, followed by another and another. At least some of them are getting away, he thought grimly. He measured the distance to his own ship, then rolled the girl off his shoulder and held her like a shield against his chest as he faced the spotlights of a converging circle of guards. He ducked around the folding chairs and tables strewn in his path as an attempt was made to barricade him. Then he concentrated on careful use of his tangle-gun charges to hamper his assailants. Six or seven more ships lifted as he made his way across the promenade, and then the open hatch of his own ship loomed nearby. With the last of his strength he hoisted the girl up into the hatchway and fell into the ship behind her, slamming the hatch shut with a clang.

It was only then that he saw the blond-haired youth *inside* the ship, aiming an automatic pistol at his chest from across the cabin.

Ben Trefon was never certain exactly what happened next, nor exactly how it happened. There had been times before when he had moved almost by instinct, assessing a situation and acting upon it in the same split second; sometimes Spacers' lives depended upon that kind of instinctive action. He knew that with the girl on the floor he had nothing to shield him, and he knew the youth's pistol could kill him. In a matter of minutes, the police outside would have the hatch pried open. The answer was clear in the same split second. His only possible safety was in space.

Without hesitation Ben slammed his hand down on the control bar, fully activating the null-grav units. In the same movement he dove across the cabin at the intruder. He heard the gun go off, a million miles away, and felt searing pain in his shoulder. Then he and the youth were rolling on the cabin floor, fighting for control of the hand that held the gun. Ben grabbed the young man's wrist, slammed the gun hand on the deck, and heard the weapon clatter across the room. The youth caught Ben in the chest with his feet, hurling him across the cabin and diving for the lost gun. Through it all the girl puffed and struggled in the tangle web, shouting encouragement to her would-be rescuer and hurling imprecations at Ben.

Suddenly, it was over. Ben's hand closed on the pistol, and he twisted to his feet, holding off his attacker with a warning gesture. The Earthman looked at him, and started for the hatchway. Ben shook his head. "Better take a look outside first," he panted.

The Earthman followed Ben's eyes to the view screen, and stared in horror. Throughout the fight the ship had been rising on its null-gravs; now Earth was a huge disc in the sky, dwindling visibly as the atomic engines took hold and hurled the ship away from the planet. The intruder shook his head helplessly as he watched his home planet receding before his eyes. "We're—in space," he said weakly. "You got away."

Ben frowned at him and, a little confused, peered at the girl. There was a similar nasal twang in their voices, and now

Ben could see a similarity in their faces too. Both of his captives had the same stubby noses, the same sandy hair and the same crop of freckles. Both were watching him with angry blue eyes. For a moment Ben didn't comprehend. Then he burst into helpless laughter.

His part of the raid had gone according to plan—almost. His orders had been to kidnap a girl, and by the moons of Jupiter he had kidnaped one.

The trouble was, he had also kidnaped her brother. And that, unfortunately, was *not* part of the plan.

3 TOO MANY PRISONERS

BEN TREFON's first overwhelming impulse was to get rid of the intruder, somehow: land again and throw him off the ship, release him in a lifeboat, do anything, but get him off the ship at any cost. He simply could not be allowed to stay. The Spacer Council would never tolerate it, and neither would common human decency. Kidnaping a woman was one thing. Kidnaping a man was something else entirely, for it violated one of the most basic laws of Spacer relations with Earthmen.

Ben gripped the pistol, glaring at his unwelcome captive and rubbing his aching shoulder. It felt as though a mule had kicked him there; actually, the discharged bullet had barely scratched the skin, but to Ben it seemed the final insult. Why did it have to happen to him? Everything going exactly as planned, the kidnaping squad working as a perfectly organized team, the Earthmen behaving exactly as predicted—and now the fly in the ointment.

Of course it was easy to see what had happened. The youth must have realized the futility of trying to stop Ben on the ground after seeing the tangle-guns doing their harmless but effective work. So he had done what must have seemed logical: waiting outside the hall until he saw where Ben was taking the girl, and taking advantage of the delaying action on the promenade to sneak aboard the ship before Ben got there. Not counting on the Spacer's resourcefulness, and not understanding how null-gravity engines worked, the youth must have thought he could prevent Ben from getting off the ground if he could only get into the ship's cabin.

Probably thought I had to crank up the motor like an air compressor, Ben thought sourly. Obviously the Earthman hadn't even known they were spaceborne until Ben had pointed to the view screen. And now, as Earth rushed away from the little ship, Ben was beginning to wish fervently that he hadn't moved quite so fast. Earth's women were a critical and necessary link in the Spacer's pattern of survival, and as long as kidnaping was the only way to recruit them, kidnaping was part of the game. If an Earth *man* came into space voluntarily, that was his own lookout, but to *force* a man out into the area of heavy cosmic radiation was something else altogether.

Because nobody knew for sure how many hours in space an Earthman could tolerate before he became finally and irrevocably a Spacer.

Staring at his unwelcome passenger, Ben searched his mind for a solution. Take him back again? Impossible now. Antiaircraft shells were bursting all around the ship, blossoming into yellow flares of violence. Every few seconds in the view screen he could see a large flare as one of the deadly ground-to-air missiles caught up with a fleeling Spacer ship, exploding on contact and blowing the ship into fragments. Twice Ben had felt his own ship jar slightly as it automatically fired its own space-to-space rockets to fight off attacking Earth missiles that had picked up his ship in their homing sights.

But something else was going on down on the planet's surface, something that didn't fit the pattern of Earth defenses against Spacer raids that Ben had learned so carefully. In half a dozen areas on the dark side of the receding planet Ben could see wave after wave of yellow sparks that flickered for a few moments and then blinked out. They looked for all the world like the rocket flares of *ships* being launched, and Ben felt the hair on the back of his neck prickle for a moment even though he knew the idea was ridiculous.

Whatever the flickering lights were, one thing was certain. He was not going to land his ship again just to unload a stowaway, not through this kind of barrage. And a lifeboat would never make it down. Maybe when they reached the Spacer orbit ship the commander would send the Earthman back after the send-off barrage had slackened and hope that he hadn't absorbed enough radiation to matter.

For the moment, though, they were stuck with each other. Ben shook his head in disgust. "You really take the stupid prize," he said to the youth. "You made your big mistake when you climbed aboard this crate."

The intruder was still staring at the view screen as though it were lying. "I don't see how it's possible," he said. "There wasn't any recoil."

"Null-grav engines don't recoil."

"And there's no way off this thing?"

"You're so right," Ben said.

On the floor of the cabin the girl had given up struggling

in the tangle web, finally realizing that if she lay perfectly still the adhesive bands stopped tightening around her arms and legs. The youth looked down at her and shook his head. "Sorry, kid," he said softly. "It looks like we're out of luck. He's pulled away clean."

Tears were forming in the girl's eyes. "You shouldn't have tried it. You should have just let me go."

"Well, it's all over now. Maybe it won't be too bad for you. And if he has any decency maybe he'll make it quick for me." He gripped the girl's shoulder for a moment, and turned to face Ben. "All right," he said. "I'm ready any time."

Ben blinked. "Ready for what?"

"Don't make it tough," the youth said desperately. "You've got the gun in your hand."

"You bet I have," Ben said. "I'm keeping it, too. Now if you'll kindly step way back, I'll break that web loose so the girl can breathe."

The Earthman didn't budge. "Look," he burst out. "You've got your prize, you've got what you came for. What more do you want?"

Ben stared at him. "You think I'm going to shoot you?"

"Well, what else? I don't want to be a guinea pig for any of your infernal Spacer experiments."

Ben snorted. "Friend, I've got trouble enough just having you aboard this ship alive. I'd have a real mess on my hands if I brought you in dead, with your sister here to testify. Now get back against that wall and shut up before I put *you* in a tangle web."

The Earthman moved back, obviously confused. Ben was angry; the intruder's words didn't make sense to him, and he didn't feel like pondering mysteries right then. Watching his captive out of the corner of his eye, he checked the control panel, adjusted the drive a fraction of a degree, and started the automatic probe signal that would establish contact with his sister ships. Then he knelt by the girl and started to cut the adherent strands of the tangle web with a small hand unit.

The web was gentle but firm, adhering to itself but not to its victim as the inactivated strands fell to the floor like strips of gauze bandage. But the girl started struggling violently the moment he came near and the webs tightened perceptibly.

"Just hold still," Ben said. "The more you fight the more they tighten up and the harder it is to get them free."

The girl only struggled harder. Ben cut a mass of strands that were holding her right arm behind her neck; then he cut the left arm loose. Half-released, the girl twisted around suddenly and bit his arm as hard as she could.

Ben jerked away. "Say, stop that!"

"Then get away from me," the girl said viciously.

"I'm only trying to release you."

"Don't you ever touch me!" the girl said. "If you so much as come near me you're going to get bitten."

Ben sat back and glared at her. The radio was chattering with incoming signals now, and the ship was jarring violently as ground-to-air missiles exploded too close for comfort. In anger Ben snatched a cleaning towel from the rack and unceremoniously stuffed it into the girl's mouth, tying the corners behind her ears. "Now go ahead and bite," he said. "I'm going to get this web off before you choke yourself in it."

She continued to struggle, making indignant noises through the towel, as Ben cut the rest of the tangle web free. He dodged flailing arms and legs as she hit him in the jaw with her knee, and then in the pit of the stomach with a bare heel. Once she was untangled, he pulled away the gag. Her teeth were chattering and she could hardly talk. "Just keep away from me," she cried, backing away from him and across the cabin toward her brother. "Just don't come near me."

There was no doubting it: the girl was terrified, almost incoherent with fear. "I'm not going to touch you," Ben said. "I'm not even going to lay a finger on you."

"Go ahead and lie," the girl shot back at him. "You can't fool me."

Ben spread his hands helplessly. "What's she afraid of?" he asked her brother.

"What do you think she's afraid of? What are we supposed to think you kidnaped her for?"

"To be a mauki, of course," Ben said.

"What's a mauki?"

"Why, a mauki's a . . . a mauki," Ben said, staring at the youth. The Earthman sounded as though he had never heard the word before, and Ben's confusion deepened. What could he say to explain, if these people were really ignorant of a mauki's place in the Spacer world? That a mauki was the wife of a Spacer? His companion in the dreadful loneliness of a Spacer's life? The mother of his boys? The proud and loyal head of the Spacer family? A mauki was all of these things, of course, and far more that was not so easy to express—at least not now, to two hostile Earth people.

At the control panel the radio chatter was becoming more insistent by the moment, and Ben's confusion gave way to suspicion. Earthmen couldn't be *this* ignorant; it had to be a trick to draw his attention away from the ship, and obviously escape had to come first. The girl was huddling against the wall, her bathing suit still damp, her lips and fingers blue. Angrily Ben threw open the hatchway to the rear compartment of the ship and pulled out a bundle of clothes. "Here," he said, tossing them to the girl. "Get out of those indecent things and get some clothes on. And let's get something straight. I'm going to move this ship out to the rendezvous point one way or another. You two can stay out of my hair while I'm doing it. If you don't, so help me I'll wrap you both in tangle webs and let you choke until we get there. Now take your choice."

The girl clutched at the clothes and disappeared into the rear compartment, slamming the hatchway behind her. Her brother relaxed and slumped down on a stool. "Anything you say," he said.

"What's your name?" Ben asked.

"Barron. Tom Barron. Her name is Joyce, and if you leave her alone I won't interfere with you."

The ship lurched again, violently. Ben caught a shock bar and sat down at the control panel. If anything, the barrage in space around them was becoming more intense, and the radio was chattering incoherently. Ben twirled the dial, searching for the command frequency that would connect him with his squad leader, so that he could signal that he was away free and clear. He found the frequency, but there was nothing but static, and a confused babble of voices. The ship was following a pre-set escape orbit for the moment; but without contact there would be no way to locate the orbit ship for rendezvous.

Five minutes later Ben was still searching for contact, without success. He could catch only fragments of chatter from the radio. Somebody trapped on the surface was broadcasting frantically for a rescue craft; somebody else with a cargo of wheat in tow between Earth and the moon had lost his null-gravs and was trying to reach a squad leader before a ground missile found him a sitting duck. From time to time a blanket of static blotted out everything. In growing alarm, Ben sent out his contact signal, but still there was no answer.

Something was wrong. By now every ship that had cleared into space should have made contact and be homing in on the orbit ship under direct radio control. This above all was critical to an effective escape; it had been rehearsed until every crewman knew the procedure to follow under every predictable circumstance from heavy barrage to merely token resistance.

Once more the ship lurched, nearly throwing Ben out of his seat. He snapped on the rear view screen in time to see one of his own air-to-air rockets flash out to intercept a pursuing Earth missile. It exploded, uncomfortably close, and the concussion wave jarred the ship again.

Suddenly, he saw something else. As the ship turned slightly in its outward course, the pale disk of Earth's moon filled the view screen. Somewhere beyond, Ben knew, the orbit ship was waiting. But now, as he started to look away, a dozen long black shadows moved out in silhouette across the moon's yellow disk like phantoms in the blackness. They were moving, and moving fast, moving outward, already far beyond his own ship.

They were not missiles. They were too large and swift for that, and they were moving into deep space beyond Earth's orbit. A moment later they had passed across the disk of the moon and were gone again into blackness, far out of range of the escaping raiders.

Only one thing was possible. They were space craft. But they looked like no ships that Spacers had ever launched.

Ben heard a swift intake of breath and saw Tom Barron staring at the view screen over his shoulder. "Did you see that?" Ben asked.

"I saw it," Tom Barron said.

"What were they?"

The Earthman's eyes were bright. "Ships," he said. "Hundreds of ships, maybe thousands. That was just one squadron."

"You mean *Earth* ships?" Ben asked incredulously.

But Tom Barron was shouting for his sister, throwing the rear compartment open in excitement. "They've launched the fleet," he cried. "Joyce, they've done it, just the way they promised! This raid must have been the trigger."

Ben Trefon stared at them. The girl was dressed in baggy Spacer fatigues, three sizes too large for her, with the cuffs and sleeves rolled up. She hugged her brother, squealing with excitement. "Did you actually *see* them?"

"No doubt about it. And if they've thrown up one squadron, that must mean the whole fleet is going out!"

"Going out where?" Ben broke in.

Tom Barron laughed. "You'll find out, soon enough. Don't worry, there won't be a one of you that doesn't find out! You think you can raid us and raid us, steal our food, steal our women—well, you'll see. You've made your last raid."

Numbly, Ben turned back to the control panel. It was incredible. Of course, Earth had always been heavily fortified for defensive action against the raiders, even though their ignorance of space techniques had made their efforts feeble. And it was true that Earth had even launched a punitive expedition from time to time in futile attempts to strike back at the Spacers. Once in a while an Earth ship had hijacked a Spacer patrol ship or a small cargo ship moving through the Asteroid Belt, shooting down the crew and gutting the ship. But these had been minor harassments to the Spacers, clumsy and foolish gestures and nothing more. There had never been anything even approaching a major assault by Earthmen against the Spacer strongholds. The very idea was ridiculous. Even if ships had somehow been built, it took crews to man them. And that was the flaw. Cruel and treacherous as they were, everyone knew that Earthmen were basically cowards when it came to space flight.

And deep space was no place for cowards.

Ben turned his attention back to his radio. The whole idea of an Earth fleet attacking Spacers was laughable. The shadows he had seen must have been missiles of some sort, some new defense maneuver. Maybe that was what his father had been thinking of when he warned about trouble on its way.

But one thing was certain: if he couldn't establish contact with his squad leader and do it soon, he would be in plenty of trouble trying to locate the orbit ship. He flipped off the automatic signal and began transmitting by hand signal, carefully probing in all quadrants of space around his ship.

Suddenly there was a response as a wave of static blotted out the blanket of overlying radio chatter. "Squad 13 here," a voice came through. "Who's contacting?"

Ben breathed a sigh of relief. "Unit 4, Squad 7," he said. "Can you hear me?"

"Just barely, but you're coming through, Unit 4. Why are you contacting?"

"No response from Squad 7 leader," Ben returned. "I'm reporting in for a track on Orbit 3."

There was a burst of static, and his contact became blotchy. He waited, then again caught the message. "Sorry, Unit 4. Squad 7 leader never got off, and the orbit ship has been hit. We're crippled ourselves."

"Do you need help?" Ben felt his hands trembling on the microphone. With the orbit ship knocked out—

"You'd never find us," Squad 13 came back. "And we're out of contact with the command ship—not even sure it's functional—so it wouldn't be any help. Follow disaster orders and get yourself out of there, boy. Any way you can. They're really coming after us."

Static broke in again, and Ben snapped off the transmitter after a vain attempt to re-contact. He took a deep breath, trying to think. Something had happened to the escape plan, something catastrophic enough to disrupt communications almost completely and throw the retreating raiders into a disaster pattern. Of course, raid plans often had to be changed somewhat to get ships and their cargoes back to the orbit ship safely, but disaster pattern meant disorganized retreat—essentially every man for himself and don't look for support.

And that could only mean that somehow this raid had really exploded a powder keg.

There was only one thing to do—to move and move fast, forgetting organized plans and heading out for the original rendezvous point by any means he could get there. If the raid still had a command ship, it would be waiting there to collect the stragglers and direct their orbits home.

Ben turned to his captives and pointed to the acceleration cots at the rear of the cabin. "Strap down," he said.

"What are you planning to do?" Tom Barron asked.

"I'm going to travel," Ben retorted. "And if you two don't want to be squashed against the bulkhead, you'd better strap down tight."

"You're wasting your time," Tom Barron said. "There's no place for you to go. You people are going to be wiped out of the sky."

"Maybe so," Ben Trefon said. "But if you think I'm going to sit around and wait for them to come and get me, you've got a surprise in store."

They strapped down.

For Ben Trefon the next few hours were a nightmare that taxed his ingenuity and navigational skill to the utmost. All of his life he had been taught navigation; it was part of a Spacer's heritage to pilot ships. He had grown from childhood with intimate contact and knowledge of the great wilderness of space that lay beyond planetary boundaries in the solar system. But he had never before been forced to put all of his knowledge to the test so abruptly or under such pressure.

He knew that until he had contacted his command ship and joined with the other raiders into some sort of organized retreat he was a sitting duck for any kind of assault weapon the

Earth forces chose to throw at him. A squadron of ships could provide a blanket of protective coverage for themselves; a single ship could depend only on its own small store of counter weapons. Now, as he accelerated to the limit of his tolerance, he was even more vulnerable because he would have so little time between detection of an assault weapon and the moment of explosion. Three times in rapid succession he "hooked" Earth missiles, each time barely getting them detonated before they struck his ship. In the blackness around him there was no sign of other ships, but the periodic flash of a contact explosion on all sides of him told him that out in the blackness other raiding ships were following the same course he was.

At one point in his wild flight his scanning radar picked up an unidentified object almost directly in his course. He dodged it, and his floodlights picked out the battered hull of another Spacer S-80 tumbling end-over-end on a witless course, with a gaping hole torn in her side—a derelict that would ultimately take up its own orbit around the Earth like a discarded first-stage shell.

Later he picked up the tentative probing of an Earth spy satellite, one of the crudely instrumented space vehicles that Earthmen had thrown up in an attempt to identify approaching Spacer craft and provide target information to assault weapons on the surface. Those vehicles had never done their job very effectively, but this one was a real threat now, pointing a sure electronic finger at Ben's ship and proving stubbornly tenacious when Ben tried to baffle its detection apparatus with maneuvering. The little S-80 lurched and bucked; Tom and Joyce Barron clutched the rails of their cots as Ben used his ship's side jets and null-grav units in combination to try to shake off his tormentor. Finally, in desperation, he fired three of his few remaining homing shells, hoping that in the confusion of objects to detect the satellite's detecting mechanism would break down. Luck was with him; one of the shells took the spy satellite out of the sky with a flash of blue light, and Ben shifted course a dozen times in the next ten minutes in hopes of losing the followup missiles that were bound to come.

His instruments had calculated the approximate rendezvous point. As the hours passed, Ben knew he must be closing in on it, yet when he broke radio silence he could hear no response except disorganized chatter. Presently even the chatter grew more sparse. He began to feel strangely alone, as though he were the only ship left in the sky.

Then, abruptly, there was a signal from close at hand and another Spacer ship hailed him. It was a twenty-man cruiser, one of the largest in the raiding fleet, and it was moving in at a tangent to Ben's S-80.

"Sound off and identify," the signal came.

"Unit 4, Squad 7," Ben returned. "Are you the command ship?"

"This is Unit 17, Squad 1," the voice came back. "We're taking command."

"What's happened?" Ben said.

"We've been booby-trapped, that's what's happened."

"But what about the orbit ship?"

"It took three shells. We had to abandon it, cargo and all. The Raid Commander is aboard here now. Better stand by for briefing."

There was a pause and some static. Then the commander's voice came across. "Unit 4? Is that Ben Trefon?"

"Yes, sir. My squad leader didn't make it, I'm told. What happened?"

"No data yet," the commander said. "All we know is that we've been hit hard. They've actually destroyed half the raiding fleet, either on the ground or spaceborne. We've lost our orbit ship and its cargo as well."

It was worse than Ben had dreamed. No raid in centuries had lost more than five per cent of its ships. "They must have known the strikepoint," he said.

"There's more to it than that," the commander returned. "I'm afraid this has been a minor skirmish, so far."

"I don't understand, sir."

"I mean we're at war," the answer came back. "Somehow they've raised an armada into space, and it's bypassed our raiding fleet altogether. Right now it's headed out for the Rings. That means they're actually going to try to fight us in space. And from the count we have of their ships, we've got a war on our hands, not just a dog fight."

For a long moment Ben was silent. It was true, then. The shadows had been ships—Earth ships. He felt a cold knot in the pit of his stomach. "What are my orders, sir?"

"Until we know what they intend to do, each ship in this raid squadron should go back to its home post, as quickly as possible. The Council and your father should be briefed without delay; that will be your job. Do you have any prisoners?"

"Too many prisoners," Ben said sourly, and reported what had happened.

"Well, I'm afraid you're hung with them until you get back

to Mars," the commander said. "This ship is already full of casualties."

"That's all right," Ben said. "I can handle them."

"Then get moving, and good luck," the fleet commander said. "Stand by for further orders when you get there. And my greetings to your father, Ben. I'm afraid he was right about this raid."

The signal snapped off, leaving unsaid the thing that loomed largest at Ben Trefon's mind. With the limitations of short-wave transmission, there was no means of swift communication between planets. That meant that if an armada of Earth ships was moving out toward the orbits of Mars and the asteroids, there would be no warning of their approach until the first fragments of the raiding fleet limped home.

But if this were really an all-out war, one of the first targets of an Earth armada would be the Spacer outposts on Mars. Swiftly Ben Trefon began plotting his course for the fastest powered flight to Mars that his fuel supply would allow. It was up to him to get word to his father and the other Mars outposts—and he knew that with all the speed he was capable of, he might still arrive too late.

4 THE BLACK BELT

SWIFT AS IT was in elapsed hours, the journey to Mars was the longest journey across space that Ben Trefon had ever experienced.

With the little scout ship's nuclear engine providing fuel for a high-energy orbit outward, and with the null-gavity units working to make high accelerations tolerable to those inside the ship's cabin, hardly more than eighteen hours passed before the great rusty red planet with its gleaming polar caps was looming large in the ship's view screens. But to Ben every hour seemed like ten, and a thousand phantoms rose in his mind as he thought of the house he had left behind on the Martian desert, defenseless unless warning came in time.

Worst of all was the simple fact that Ben Trefon could not comprehend the idea of a full-scale war between Earthmen and Spacers, no matter how hard he tried. His mind balked at the thought; there was nothing in his experience, nor in his knowledge of Spacer history, that could account for such a thing being possible. As a result, he had the continuing feeling that it wasn't really true at all, that it was merely a bad dream from which he would awaken at any moment. And the more he considered the idea the more incredible it became.

Of course he knew of the long centuries of animosity that had existed between the people who lived on the surface of the mother planet and the wandering band of outcasts who made their homes in space, on the outer planets or in the Asteroid Belt. He also knew that this animosity had flared into violence from time to time, ever since the beginning of the Spacers' long exile from Earth. The periodic raids on the mother planet, so critical to the Spacers' survival, never failed to whip the Earthmen into heights of frustrated rage, all the more intense because their efforts to fight off the raiders proved so feeble. This rage was reflected in the viciousness and cruelty Earthmen displayed on the rare occasions when they attempted to send out retaliatory missions against their tormentors. Space ships had been destroyed, men killed and maukis taken back to Earth in chains during those skirmishes, but to the Spacers the occasional Earth pirates had been nothing more than one of the unpleasant facts of their life in space, just another adverse condition that the Spacer clan had had to put up with in order to survive in their nomadic life.

But the Spacers' long familiarity with space, their skill in navigation and their knowledge of interplanetary spaceways were also facts of life—facts that had given them unquestioned superiority beyond the limits of Earth's gravitational field. Another fact of life was the horror with which Earthmen had always viewed contact with space, the dread of space travel that had always filled their minds. Space had always been the Spacers' province; if they could not return to Earth, they had always felt themselves impregnable beyond her surface, and that impregnability had been demonstrated time and again when Earth ships had ventured out. It had been argued that nothing short of mass insanity would ever drive Earthmen to try to dislodge them from Space by force.

And now, with the fact of such a war staring them in the face, they were caught without warning. Of course, if it were true, there could be no question about the outcome of such a war, Ben Trefon thought. No ships from Earth, manned by Earthmen, could really hope to press an invasion of the Spacers' domain successfully. But cruel and treacherous as Earthmen were, they might certainly wreak havoc before they were driven back to quarters.

Ben turned over these thoughts as he continued plotting the finer details of the ship's course toward Mars. In a way, it was comforting to believe that Spacers were impregnable, but something in the idea caught in his mind and left him vaguely uneasy. If Earthmen *had* gone mad in their hatred of Spacers, there was no sign of it in his two Earth captives. Nor did they seem particularly formidable, or even evil, now that they were convinced he meant them no immediate harm. If anything, he reflected, these two seemed more stunned than treacherous, more terrified than cruel.

Yet as far as he could tell, there was nothing about Tom and Joyce Barron that made them different from other Earthmen. As brother and sister who could hardly be more than a year apart in age, they seemed very close; try as he would, Ben could not even imagine what it might be like to have a sister, but it seemed to be a very comfortable relationship. Until they had contacted the command ship they had been talking together quietly just as brothers might talk, and half the time they each seemed to know what the other was thinking.

On questioning them, Ben learned that their father was a colonel in the Earth civil defense garrison, commander of the guard units protecting the southern part of the metropolis of Chicago. Even Tom and Joyce did not know what part he might have in the launching of the Earth armada, although they seemed sure that he had known about it. Although they made no attempt to conceal their anger and frustration at being caught aboard a Spacer ship, neither could they conceal their curiosity when Ben pulled away from the command ship, set the ship moving, and began plotting orbit with the aid of the ship's computer.

"What are you planning to do?" Tom Barron wanted to know. "What's going to happen to us?"

"You heard what the man said," Ben said bluntly. "We're at war. Your ships are moving out to attack our space outposts. So that makes you enemy aliens aboard this ship, and I'm responsible for you until I can get you interned somewhere."

"You mean we just have to stay aboard this ship forever?" Joyce Barron asked.

"Believe me, I don't like it any better than you do," Ben said. "But for the time being we're stuck with it whether we like it or not."

"Well, are you going to lock us up somewhere?"

Ben looked at the girl. "That's up to you," he said. "We have to count on this ship to keep us alive and get us where we want to go. But I can't operate the ship if I have to be watching you two for tricks all the time."

Tom Barron shrugged. "It seems to me that we don't have much choice about it," he said. "You won't be operating this ship very long anyway, with our fleet in the sky. So we won't interfere with you."

Ben studied Tom Barron's face. "I've heard that an Earthman's word isn't worth much," he said.

"It'll stand up to a Spacer's word any time," Joyce said hotly.

"Well, it doesn't really matter. You wouldn't get far trying to operate this ship, and even if you could you'd be blown out of space before you could land it on Earth. There's no place out here for you to go without knowing where and how, so I guess I can trust you for the moment."

Joyce Barron's face flushed. "Maybe you want a written treaty," she said.

"No, but I want some things understood," Ben said. "Call them rules of the ship, if you wish." He ticked them off on his fingers. "First, you keep your hands off the controls. You could kill us all in about ten seconds flat if you happened to pull the wrong switch. Second, you keep away from the radio. This is a Spacer ship, and from what I've heard any of your Earth ships we run into are likely to shoot first and ask questions later. So we won't break radio silence unless we have to. Third, you do what you're told to do and don't argue. I've got to know where you are and what you're doing all the time, in case anything were to go wrong with the ship. Okay?"

The Barrons looked at each other, and then nodded. "Okay," Tom said. "But you might tell us a couple of things. We don't even know your name."

"You can call me Ben Trefon," Ben said.

"And you were—born in space?"

"Of course," Ben said, puzzled.

"There, I told you," Tom said to his sister.

"Yes, but you still can't be sure," she said. Then she shook her head and whispered something in her brother's ear.

"Well, there's one way to find out," Tom said.

"No, no, not now—"

"Yes, now," Tom told her. "We might as well know now as later."

"Whatever are you talking about?" Ben asked.

"Let me feel your hand," Tom challenged.

"My *hand?"*

"Hold it out—if you're not afraid to."

Ben held out his hand. To his amazement, the Earthman closed his eyes tight, reached out and touched the outstretched hand, felt the fingers and wrist, and patted his arm from wrist to elbow. Then with eyes still closed he reached up and touched Ben's face. Finally he opened his eyes with a sigh of relief. "It's just as I told you," he said to Joyce. "It's all right."

The girl looked crestfallen. "And you're the only one here?" she asked Ben. "I mean, you don't have any other—crew—aboard?"

"Well, what do you expect? A hold full of monsters?" Ben turned away in disgust. "I don't know what you're looking for, but I for one am getting hungry, and I have course corrections to make. Why don't you break out some food?"

Following his directions, Joyce found the cupboard panel that opened out into a tiny galley. After experimenting with the heat-pump stove that worked from the ship's heating system, she got to work heating up some canned stew and some biscuits as Tom followed Ben back to the control panel. A few moments later their mutual uneasiness was momentarily forgotten as they munched hungrily, and Ben began the complex task of plotting the final course adjustments for the run to Mars.

Tom watched him curiously as he took the plotting cards out of the computer slot, made his calculations on the backs of them, taped the new data back into the computer and waited for the revised cards to be returned. Finally curiosity won. "What are you doing with that machine?" Tom asked.

"Correcting our course," Ben said. "The basic orbit was easy, just a matter of matching fuel against time and pointing the ship in the right direction. But we have to have the fine adjustments before we go into high gear. Once we're on nuclear drive and really accelerating, even a minor course change might burn out the null-gravs and then we'd really be in the soup."

"I see," said Tom, who didn't see at all. "But don't you have to have starting co-ordinates before you can plot an orbit?"

"Of course. You can't hope to make connection with any point in space unless you know where you're starting from."

Tom glanced up at the view screen. They were far beyond the range of the Earth ground-to-air barrage now, and all that was visible was a vast expanse of blackness peppered with stars. "So how can you ever tell where you are?"

The question seemed a little foolish to Ben. "We're in the cabin of a ship, naturally."

"But where's the ship?"

"Relative to what?" Ben said. "Relative to Earth? If that's what you mean, I don't know and couldn't care less. The computer could tell me, of course, if I had to find out. The important thing is where the ship is, relative to where we're going right now. I had to establish that before I could even start this orbit. I also had to decide whether I wanted a long, low-energy orbit or a fast, high-energy course. Now I've got time to pin down the details and see just how fast we can afford to travel to intersect Mars's orbit in the shortest possible elapsed time."

"You mean you can pick your travel time?" Tom asked incredulously.

"Within the ship's energy limits, yes. We have so much energy potential in the reactors. If we picked the highest-energy orbit to Mars that our fuel supply would allow, we could probably be landing within forty minutes including acceleration and deceleration—except that the acceleration we'd have to undertake would burn out the null-grav units in ten seconds and we'd be smashed into a pulp ten seconds later."

Tom Barron frowned. "But I thought your antigravity generators were only good for landing and taking off from planetary surfaces."

"Why? Why should they be limited to that? You measure acceleration in gravities, don't you? And a human being without protection in a space ship can only tolerate a few gravities for a few minutes. Without null-G this trip would take us months, and even then we'd have to tolerate weighing four hundred pounds apiece for about half the time. Null-G takes the weight off us and puts it on the ship's generators, which cut into the total fuel supply but still give us speed. So we balance fuel available against the maximum acceleration gravities the null-G units can handle, and that gives us the highest-energy orbit the ship is capable of and tells us our travel time. See what I mean?"

"I guess so," Tom said dubiously. "But I still don't see how you can ever locate yourself definitely relative to anything when you move around the way you do."

"Well, obviously I have to have a baseline somewhere. We use our central dispatching station at Asteroid Central as a baseline. Otherwise we just plain couldn't navigate in space. The computer at Central keeps running tabs on every known chunk of orbiting land mass in the solar system, relative to itself in its own orbit around the sun. So at any given instant the main computer can tell where each of the planets is in its orbit, how fast it is moving at the time, how rapidly it's accelerating or decelerating in its orbit at the moment, and where Asteroid Central is in relation to it. That way any ship that leaves Asteroid Central can blank its own computer and file in its baseline co-ordinates at that particular point in time and space. It just lifts that chunk of information from the main computer. And then, to get a fix later the pilot just has to calculate back. Of course, every movement the ship makes after leaving Central is automatically filed into its own computer."

Tom peered at the shiny bank of dials on the control panel. "That must be quite some little computer," he said.

"It has to be. Its capacity is pretty amazing, but the pilot still has to do some of the work. On Asteroid Central the main computer does it all." Ben scribbled once more on a card, punched the feeder tape running down into the computer, waited a few moments until the return card dropped down in the slot, and finally began setting the ship's controls. Then he rechecked the figures, and shook his head. "It's going to be slow," he said. "We're already fifteen degrees out of opposition with Mars, and losing ground all the time. We can do it in another seventeen hours if we accelerate for fourteen of them, and if the null-gravs don't burn out when we try to slow down in three. But that's the best we can do." He made some final adjustments in the dials. "That should do it. Now here we go."

He threw the drive switches, and sank back in the control chair with a sigh. There was a low-pitched rumble from somewhere in the rear of the ship, and a slight vibration beneath their feet; otherwise, nothing seemed to have happened. For a moment or two the star pattern in the view screen shifted slowly, then fixed again. The ship seemed to be standing still in the blackness.

Joyce joined them at the control panel as Ben was setting the dials. Now she said, "What's wrong?"

"Not a thing," Ben Trefon said.

"But nothing's happening, we're just standing still."

Ben grinned. "You think so, eh?" He braced his feet, hooked his arm around a shock bar on the control panel, and then turned the null-gravity dial a fraction of a degree. Abruptly he felt the acceleration tugging at his arm; Tom and Joyce Barron began staggering back across the cabin as though drawn by a giant vacuum cleaner. Ben snapped the dial back sharply, and his prisoners jerked forward again, fighting to keep their balance.

"We're moving, all right," Ben assured them. "If the null-G's weren't working now, our acceleration would be quietly squeezing you through the rear bulkhead into the engine room, so you'd better just pray that nothing goes wrong with our generators."

Visibly impressed, Joyce Barron stared out the view screen. "So we're going to Mars." She hesitated. "Are there any laboratories there?"

"Just some observation labs, and the Botanical Experiment Station. But we're not going there. We're going to my home."

Joyce looked startled. "You mean you live on Mars?"

"Sometimes."

"But I thought you people lived in space ships!"

"We do—sometimes. But you can't grow food on a space ship. You can't raise children there, either, or forge tools, or manufacture ships. Spacers have homes all over the solar system. It so happens that the House of Trefon has always been on Mars."

"Trefon," the girl said thoughtfully. "I never heard a name like that before."

Ben laughed. "Maybe that's because there isn't any. I mean, officially. That's just my short name. On the records I'm Benjamin Ivanovitch Trefonovsky, but that's too clumsy to use. Ben Trefon works much better."

The girl was looking at him with distaste. "Then you must be descended from the Russian traitors," she said contemptuously.

"From the Russian space garrison, yes. From traitors, no. The Trefons have never been traitors."

"They betrayed their government during the Great War, didn't they?" Joyce Barron said indignantly. "Everybody knows that. They conspired with the American and British traitors and sold out their countries when they were needed the most."

"They refused to burn their home planet to a cinder, that's true," Ben said slowly. "Maybe that's your idea of treachery. But if it hadn't been for the peace in space, there'd be nothing left on Earth at all, *nothing*. You wouldn't be alive and neither would anybody else. But I don't suppose you'd believe that, with all the lies your government tells you."

"You can't deny historical fact," the girl exclaimed.

"I can, if it's written by liars," Ben retorted angrily. "I've heard about the lies they teach you on Earth. Well, that's your concern. You can go ahead and believe them if you want, but don't try to tell them to me."

He turned away with a strange feeling of weariness and disgust. It was the old, old argument he had heard so many times before, and it was just as false and evil now as it ever was. Lies, officially presented as history and drummed into their heads from childhood on until they accepted them blindly and wouldn't even consider that they might not be the truth. It must be true, Ben thought, what he had heard about the vicious propaganda that all Earthmen had thrown at them constantly; here were two in his own ship spouting it back at him. It was no wonder that there was no end to the bitterness between Earthmen and Spacers.

But he knew that there was no sense arguing the question now. He didn't really care if his prisoners thought he was descended from traitors—why should he care *what* they thought? They were prisoners of war now, and nothing more, and he had other things more important to worry about.

He checked the controls, rechecked the pre-calculated orbit to be sure the ship was following precisely, and then fought down a yawn. "Look," he said to Tom, "I haven't slept for two days. The ship is on automatic so it won't require checking for a while. I'm going to try to rest, and you two would be smart to get some sleep too. We may not have much chance when we get where we're going."

He threw himself down on an acceleration cot, feeling the vibration of the ship's engines throbbing through his body as the ship moved out in the great arc that would take him to Mars and home. His body ached, and he desperately wanted to sleep, but rest was not easy. He could let his body sag and relax, but he could not throw off the vast weight of apprehension that lay on his mind, plaguing him as he thought of his father's last words to him, and of the House of Trefon on the desert plateau above the Great Rift on Mars.

He had to get warning there in time. Anything else was unthinkable. He thought of the long history of the House of Trefon, of the pride and honor of his grandfather and his father in that house and of the unselfish leadership they had provided the Spacer clan. If the House of Trefon were to fall to an invading fleet from Earth, far more would be lost than a few lives and a house on the Martian desert. . . .

He forced the thought out of his mind angrily, and thought instead of the happy days he had spent in his father's house, the long exploratory trips they used to take down into the Rift, or north to the dessicated ruins of the Martian cities, the silent monuments of the race that had once lived on that planet before its water had gone, so very different from human beings and yet so strangely similar, from the evidence they had left behind them. As a race the Martians had perished, unable to escape a dying planet and unable to survive upon it. And eons later, another race of creatures on the blue-green planet closer to the sun had been threatened by extinction by their own hands and had survived only because a few of them had discovered a larger challenge than their own ambitions.

Ben thought of Joyce Barron's scornful words, and again anger rose in his mind. He knew the true story of the Spacers' exile, of course. Every Spacer did. It was recorded in the log books of the earliest space garrisons that existed before the Great War. Parts of it had been pieced together from official documents; much had been handed down from father to son. Ben had heard the story time and again in the songs and ballads of the maukis, and that more than anything had driven it into the very fiber of his mind, for the mournful chants of the maukis were one of the most powerful forces that bound all Spacers together in their loneliness.

So Ben Trefon knew that there had been a time when Earth had been divided against itself in a bitter war. For more than a century the two greatest nations on Earth had pitted themselves against each other, building horrible weapons and mounting massive artillery against the day when nuclear war would come. Outposts in space had become an important part of that race for armament, as the great powers competed to mount manned satellites in orbit around the Earth, armed with weapons powerful enough to smash the planet into fragments. Earth's moon was explored and turned into a fortress; Mars and Venus were probed and even the asteroids were explored and exploited for the radioactive riches they contained.

A nuclear war, sooner or later, had seemed inevitable. In the council halls and government strongholds on Earth the jousting had become more and more desperate, until the final blow seemed only a matter of time. By then both sides knew that the final blow would come from the space garrisons, and both sides on Earth had built their hopes and their defenses in the powerful forces beyond the planet's surface.

But in space an incredible thing happened. For those early pioneers in space, violent danger and sudden death were constant companions. Survival alone was a never ending, unremitting battle against fearful odds. To those men food, shelter, oxygen and water were the vital issues, and the ideas that divided the nations on Earth in their remoteness seemed petty and quibbling to these men who fought their hearts out merely to survive. It was not so strange that an *esprit de corps* grew up among them, a sense of closeness in the face of death, a common loyalty that seemed to override the importance of the nations of their birth and the politics of their governments. Nor was it strange that this common loyalty to themselves as men brought with it a new kind of sanity and opened their eyes to values their governments on Earth had long forgotten.

They realized that they held in their hands weapons that could wipe their home planet barren of life. At first as individuals and then in frank conspiracy they realized that these weapons must never be used. So, when the moment of truth arrived in the councils on Earth, and the Earth forces delivered their blows at each other, expecting the massive backing of their garrisons in space, the men in those garrisons drew together shoulder to shoulder and withheld the devastating attack they were expected to deliver.

There had surely been a conspiracy, Ben Trefon thought, but a conspiracy to draw the teeth of the warring factions on Earth. The Earth councils had raged and threatened and pleaded, and finally had gone on to fight their war as best they could, but its force was blunted as the space garrisons refused to deliver the suicidal blow. After the dust of the war had settled, those brave men in space reaped the reward of their deed as the councils on Earth turned against them in frustration and hatred. It was a bitter reward, and time did not change it. Branded as traitors, they were exiled from the planet of their birth, driven back when they attempted to come home, forced to take up a lonely, wandering life in the great emptiness of space beyond the boundaries of Earth.

This was the history of the Spacers that every Spacer knew: the history of a group of people cast out and reviled, with cruel injustice, by a homeland that became more bitter as the years passed. And now, Ben thought sleepily, injustice was heaped upon injustice, for the outcasts could not even be left alone to live in space! There was no doubt in his mind that this was the true account of Space history . . . yet a nagging question remained that he could not quite answer. If this was the whole truth, then his prisoners had to be wrong. And yet he had the strange feeling that Tom and Joyce Barron, born and raised on Earth, really believed that he and his father's house were beneath contempt, the offspring of pirates and traitors who deserved nothing more than total extermination.

And he wondered, as he drifted to sleep, if any of them, Earthmen *or* Spacers, really knew the *whole* truth.

He awoke with a start, the alarm bell clanging in his ears. He had had a terrible dream; a huge black space ship had been attacking, firing wave after wave of missiles that were weaving their way inexorably toward him as his own defensive shells jammed in their tubes and refused to fire. Now he leaped from the cot and crossed the cabin in three steps, his hands on the missile controls before his eyes were completely open.

But there was no ship in the view screen. Instead, he saw a great ruddy disc growing larger by the minute, its polar caps glistening. Ben glanced at the chronometer; he had slept almost twelve hours, and now the alarm was signaling that deceleration was finished and the ship was ready to move into braking orbits around Mars.

Ben sighed with relief and snapped off the alarm. Between planets the ship required little attention, correcting its position automatically against the designated orbit and decelerating at precisely the rate necessary to bring ship's orbit and planet's orbit together to permit landing. But landing maneuvers required human skill and judgment. Only in the most extreme emergency would a pilot attempt to plot a landing for his ship without his own hands on the controls, for a few feet of miscalculation could make the difference between a safe landing and a heap of burning rubble on the desert sand.

Now the Barrons were up, crowding behind Ben as he set the controls for his first braking orbit. He felt the drag of the outer reaches of the planet's atmosphere against the ship, and peered at the disk in the view screen, searching for the landmarks he knew so well.

Suddenly, Ben Trefon felt a chill settle in his chest. In some indefinable way, the surface of the planet looked odd, changed somehow since the last time he saw it. He searched for the shiny dome of the Botanical Experiment Station as he braked in closer to the surface. It was the first landmark he always spotted on a Mars landing, but now he could not find it. As the ship moved across the dark side of the planet, it seemed that there were a dozen glowing red patches visible in the blackness, an eerie succession of ghostly lights he had never seen before.

As he approached the twilight zone, he dipped the ship down sharply. Now details began to appear, and Ben forgot his passengers as he gripped the controls, almost crying out at the ruin he saw spread out before his eyes across the planet surface.

There was a great gaping scar, still smoking, where the experiment station had once stood. Ahead he saw another scar, and another. He searched for the Great Rift and found it, but the straight, clean line he had always seen now looked ragged and broken. He was still searching for the plateau that lay above it when the ship crossed again to the dark side and moved down into its final landing arc.

Stunned, Ben Trefon watched for the bright side again. Once more he found the Rift, saw the blackened crater where another Spacer house had stood. Then he saw the familiar landmarks, the low plateau rising between the Rift and the mountains, and his eyes confirmed what he had seen fleetingly on the last sweep.

He snapped on the null-gravity units, tapped the forward jets, and eased the ship down on a hillock overlooking the plateau. Dust rose around the ship as it settled, but Ben did not see it. He was climbing into a pressure suit before the generators stopped whining, and moments later he stepped down from the exit lock and felt the sand crunch beneath his feet as he walked to the brow of the hill.

Below him, the House of Trefon was a smoking ruin. Fragments of plastic dome stood shattered like broken glass in the sunlight. One of the great stone arches still stood among the fragments of the others. The hangar area was a glowing crater; in the back of the house the Council chamber was split open in a heap of rubble. The cold wind sweeping down from the north flapped a colored curtain back and forth against a ruined window frame. Except for this there was no movement, no breath of life, nothing but silence and desolation.

Numbly, Ben turned back to the ship. The radiation counter was clicking in his ear: that meant there was still activity in the craters, but the level was low. All the same, he would need a shielded suit before approaching closer.

Inside the ship he pulled off the helmet, and then stopped dead. Tom and Joyce Barron were staring at the view screen. They looked up at him, and their eyes reflected horror and disbelief. "Where are we?" Tom said. "Why are we stopping here? What is that out there?"

The numbness seemed to reach to Ben's fingertips. "That's our destination," he said through the tightness in his throat. "Still hot. Still smoking. Take a good look."

"But you said we were going to your home—" Joyce's voice trailed off.

Rage exploded in Ben Trefon's mind. With a sweep of his arm he tore open a locker, hauled out heavy shielded suits, dumped them at the feet of his prisoners. "Go ahead, put them on," he said. "Don't worry, you won't have to get your feet dirty. And you won't get too close to the hot places, I'll see to that. Well, what are you waiting for? You wouldn't want to miss this. Put on the suits. I'll take you on a private tour of the greatest house on Mars."

It was a grim party that made its way down the slope to the edge of the ruins. Ben took the lead, his rage subsiding to a cold white flame. The Barrons followed close behind him. He skirted the obviously hot craters in the hangar area and moved on into the rubble-strewn entry hall. Fragments of the wall were still standing. Great chunks of the tile floor had been thrown up at angles, but Ben picked a careful path through the ruin. Some parts of the house were still recognizable, but his family's living quarters had taken a shell directly. Not even a fragment remained.

Ben stopped. There was no point to going on. There was not even a stir of life, no sign of human activity. Nothing could have survived such an onslaught. The house had literally been pounded into the ground. Ben knew without looking that he would find no survivors.

In his earphones he heard a choked sob, and the girl said, "I'm going back to the ship." Something in her voice brought a wave of shame to Ben's mind. Irrationally he had been blaming the Barrons personally for his loss, rubbing their noses in it. "Yes, go back," he said. "There's nothing here for you to see." He took her arm, guided her across the rubble and out of the danger area. "Go on up and wait in the ship," he told her gently. "We won't be long."

Tom started to follow her, but Ben caught his arm. "I'm going to need some help. You'd better stay."

The Earthman's eyes were bright with suspicion. "What do you think you're going to do here?"

"My father was in this house," Ben said. "We have to be sure there are no survivors. And there's something I have to look for."

Reluctantly Tom followed him. For almost an hour they searched the rubble in vain. Maybe some of the people in the house had been evacuated, somehow, but Ben found the ruined shell of his father's cruiser lying at the edge of the hangar crater. He looked no further. He knew that his father would never have left the house, no matter what the emergency, as long as anyone else remained to be evacuated.

Later he knew that he would try to piece together the details of his father's death, try to imagine what had happened here from the first moment of warning until the last blow was struck. But for the time being Ben simply accepted it, numbly, as he accepted the ruin of the house. Just one thing burned in his mind now, one thing that had to be done.

He began searching for the stairs that led down to the vault. His father's words were fresh in his mind; there was something there, something that was now his responsibility.

With Tom's help he found a way down the sandstone passage that led to the armored vault. It took half an hour of work to clear the passage of rubble, but they managed it. One side of the vault had been caved in under the force of a direct hit, and part of the lead shielding in the ceiling sagged, but the main archives were intact, the repository of Spacer records, deeds, documents and other official papers. If only they had come down here, Ben thought, some of them might have survived. But he knew that no Spacers under attack would ever think of hiding in the ground. For them space would seem the only safe place.

Finally they reached the family vault. The mechanism of the door had been damaged by the bombardment, but it responded to Ben's handprint and the door opened with a groan. Inside, on a steel table, they found a sealed pouch, and a hand-scribbled note on a piece of gray paper.

Ben picked up the note, recognized his father's hasty scrawl. "These are yours," the note said, "to guard with your life and pass on to your children. The belt is your authority and identification, to be worn until its contents are demanded. The tape is also to be passed on, although its words mean nothing now. One day you may understand it. These things are yours; guard them well, and good luck, my son."

Inside the pouch were a belt and a spool of tape. The belt was black, a strip of elastic mesh with a capsule enclosed in the fabric. The capsule was the size of an egg, smooth and silvery as Ben removed it from its pocket in the belt. It felt metallic in his hand, and yet it was strangely warm to the touch. He replaced it in the belt and ran the belt around his waist. The elastic seemed to clasp him as though it welcomed a carrier.

"What is it?" Tom Barron said.

"I don't know," Ben replied. "My father wore it as long as I can remember. I always thought it was a gift from my mother, but now that I think of it I'm sure Dad told me once that it was handed down by my grandfather." Ben paused, trying to draw forth a memory that had been buried completely for years. "Once when I was very small Dad showed me these things—the belt, and the tape too. He told me that the men of the House of Trefon were some kind of guardians, 'Keepers of the keys' was the way he put it, but he never told me what we were guarding."

Tom pointed to the spool on the table. "What about the tape?"

"That's part of it, too." Ben crossed the room and slid a tape player out from the wall. The tape was an ancient one, wrinkled and frayed as though played many times. It was an old style tape spool with open edges, but it fit into the player. Ben threaded it, turned the switch, and waited as the tape slowly began to unwind.

At first there was just a crackle of static. Then, suddenly, they heard a voice, a woman's voice, singing.

It was a mauki chant. It was the first time Tom Barron had ever heard a mauki sing; for a moment he dismissed it as foolishness at a time like this, just a tape recording of somebody singing a song. But then he stopped, and turned, and listened, suddenly shivering in the half-lighted room.

For Ben Trefon the voice brought back a flood of childhood memories, and a wave of loneliness that was almost unbearable. For as long as he could remember Spacer women had always sung; it was one of the things that made them maukis. Of course there were many kinds of mauki songs, but most familiar were the laments, the haunting songs of grief and loss, half ballad and half chant, that never really told a story yet always conveyed with overwhelming force their message of Spacer hopes and Spacer longings.

And this tape was a mauki chant, so familiar and so compelling that it brought tears to Ben's eyes. Yet, in some ways it was different from any mauki chant he had ever heard before.

He had listened for several minutes before he realized that he was not understanding the words.

There was no question that words were being sung. They were clear and distinct in every syllable, and they seemed to match perfectly the eerie minors and halftones of the lament. For a moment Ben thought his ears were playing tricks on him, because the words were almost familiar, almost understandable—but not quite. He had the feeling that if only he could listen more intently he might be able to distinguish them, but even as he listened he realized that this was not so. Nor was he the only one—he saw the look of wonder and confusion on Tom's face and knew the Earthman could not distinguish the words either.

A long while later the singing faded into silence, and the two stood staring at each other. Without a word Ben rewound the tape and played it again. Still the words remained obscure.

"I don't understand it," Tom Barron said finally, breaking the silence.

"Neither do I," Ben said.

"But what language is it?"

"I never heard it before in my life. But this is one of the keys my father spoke of."

"But what good is it? What does it mean, and why is it so important for you to guard it?"

"I don't know," Ben said thoughtfully. "At least, not now."

He took the tape out of the player, wrapped it carefully in the pouch and slipped it into his pocket. "If the tape and the belt are keys my father was keeping, what does that suggest to you?"

"That there's a lock somewhere that they will open," Tom Barron said.

"Yes," Ben Trefon said softly. He stood silent for a moment, still hearing the mauki chant ringing in his ears. Then he shook his head and started for the door. "Yes," he said again. "For once I think you are one hundred per cent right."

5 THE PHANTOM SHIP

IT WAS ALMOST dark when Ben Trefon and Tom Barron returned to the little scout ship. As the sun sank below the ridge of hills on the horizon the sky had turned a glorious purple; now it was fading to velvet black, pierced by a myriad of stars. Already the cold night wind was boring down from the north as the temperature of the thin Martian atmosphere plummeted, and already the first sprinkling of red dust and sand whirled in eddies around the ruins of the once great house as the desert moved in to reclaim its own.

Joyce had food prepared for them, and Ben Trefon and his two prisoners ate in gloomy silence. None of them had any appetite. Ben sat apart from the Barrons, staring through the view screen at the darkening landscape.

When it was too dark to see any more, he turned away. "So that's the end of it," he said with an edge of bitterness in his voice. "For three hundred years that house has stood there. It was built the hard way, with muscle and sweat. None of your great building machines to help. The foundations were chiseled and blasted out of bedrock, and the stone for the walls was carried up from the rim of the Rift and laid in the walls piece by piece. Three hundred years, and now a heap of rubble."

The Barrons joined him in front of the view screen. Since the visit to the vault Tom had been strangely subdued, hardly talking even to his sister, and the girl's face was pale.

"So that was your home," she said finally.

Ben nodded.

"I didn't believe you, at first. It just didn't seem possible that Spacers would have homes. I always thought of them as wandering from place to place like the Arabs on our own deserts."

"There isn't so much difference," Ben Trefon said. "After all, the space between the planets is a desert, a lot more barren than any desert you've ever seen on Earth. And even your Arabs have oases, don't they? Places they return to, places to stop and rest, places with water and shade and comfort." He pointed toward the ruins of the house below. "I can remember the great gatherings we had in those halls," he said. "Spacers from all over the solar system would stop here, and they would always be welcome. The women were always singing here, and the children had plenty of room to run." Ben smiled. "I can remember when I was very small, maybe five or six, I found one of the old Martian tunnels, down there in the Rift. It must have run for miles back into these hills. I searched and searched, because I'd heard stories of underground chambers filled with diamonds and guarded by dragons. Of course, those were only stories—the chambers were used as water reservoirs to provide moisture for the crops when the runoff was over, back when the Martians were here. They must have been a brave people, but bravery wasn't enough. They finally died. And now we're gone, too."

"I'm sorry," Joyce Barron said softly.

"Why?"

"Because you've lost your home. I—I'm not sure our pilots knew what they were destroying."

"But why should you be sorry?" Ben said. "You should be proud. This must have been their first objective, and your ships did a fine job on it. It looks to me like they made a clean sweep, blotted out everything they could see."

"It just doesn't seem right," Joyce said.

"Why not? This is your war. Why be sorry when you win the first battle hands down?"

"But your people forced the war," the girl said.

"How?" Ben Trefon said bitterly. "How did we force it? We tried and tried to make peace with you, but you wouldn't listen. Can you blame us for trying to stay alive? Did you ever see us killing and maiming and pounding cities to rubble on any of our raids? We could have, easily enough, but we never did."

"You hadn't done that *yet,*" Tom Barron broke in. "But we knew it was coming sooner or later. That was obvious to everybody. We knew it was just a matter of time, until you had your war machines finished and your army of monsters trained and ready to invade us. What else could we do but fight back, when we knew that was coming?"

"What are you talking about?" Ben said.

"The Spacer invasion, of course. You didn't really think that we would stand by and wait for you to unleash your monster hordes against us, to slaughter us or turn us into slaves? Do you really blame us for turning and fighting?"

Ben Trefon stared at the sandy-haired youth. There was no mistaking the utter sincerity in his voice, but the words made no sense. "Monster hordes? Invasion? What are you saying?"

Tom Barron shook his head angrily. "Look, can't we stop pretending now? We know what you people have been doing all these years. We know what you've been planning, we've known it for decades. So why try to pretend it isn't true now? We're your prisoners, we can't do anything, but at least we can be honest."

"But I'm not pretending," Ben exploded. "I don't even understand what you're saying."

"Are you going to pretend that you haven't been raiding us for centuries?"

"Well, of course we've been raiding you."

"And stealing our women?"

"That's true, too," Ben said.

"You bet it's true. Spacers have kidnaped women on every raid they've ever made. Thousands and thousands of girls, and not one of them ever came back."

Ben Trefon scratched his jaw. "What's that got to do with monsters?"

Tom snorted in disgust. "We may not know much about space navigation, but we aren't stupid. We've had enough radiation accidents and nuclear wars to know about the mutants that result, and we know about the radiation in space. You've got to be using Earth women for something, and we can put two and two together."

Ben stared at him, wondering if he had heard right. His first impulse was to laugh, but the desperate sincerity in Tom's voice stopped him. He isn't making this up as he goes along, Ben thought. He actually believes what he's saying. Suddenly a dozen puzzling little things began to make sense: Tom Barron's desperate move to try to prevent his sister's kidnaping, his obvious suspicion of Ben, his questions about laboratories on Mars and his assumption that Ben would kill him when he was first captured—suddenly it began to make a horrible kind of sense.

"Wait a minute," Ben Trefon said. "Wait a minute now. Tell me again so I'm sure I've got this straight. What do you think we are?"

"You mean you yourself?"

Ben shook his head. "I mean Spacers in general."

"We know what you are," Tom Barron said.

"Do you think we're human?"

Tom hesitated. "Human, yes. But changed. Without any

atmosphere to protect you, you get hard doses of cosmic radiation, and that makes changes. Some of the Earthmen who went into space and came home again were changed, and had monsters for children."

"What kind of monsters?" Ben broke in.

"Creatures with two heads, creatures that could hypnotize just by looking at you, creatures that could read minds, I don't know what else. The government never did publish deatils."

"And you thought I was a monster in disguise," Ben said. "That was why you wanted to feel my hands and face."

"I thought it was possible," Tom said stiffly. "Hypnosis can blind people and make them see things that aren't really there."

Ben nodded grimly. It fit, every bit of it. A simple truth, but completely misinterpreted, twisted and distorted by the telling and retelling until it was turned into utter falsehood. "And these laboratories," Ben went on. "Tell me about them. Where are they supposed to be, and what's supposed to be happening in them?"

Tom Barron shook his head. "Nobody on Earth has ever found out where they are, but we know *what* they are. You'd have to have breeding places for your monsters, places to experiment until you could breed the kind of invasion army you wanted." The Earthman's voice was bitter. "I don't know why I'm wasting my time talking. You already know all this. But at least you seem to be halfway human—can't you see how we feel?" He looked up at Ben. "Think about it for a minute. Think how you'd feel, living down there, if you knew that any minute, any hour, any day or year, raiders might be coming down to carry off your own sister to breed monsters with. Think how you'd feel!"

There was a long pause as Ben looked from Tom Barron to his sister and back again. He could see the truth now, so simple that it was ridiculous, yet twisted into a horrible nightmare in his prisoners' minds. He shook his head slowly. "I'm sorry," he said, "but I can't."

"Can't what?"

"I can't imagine how I'd feel, no matter how hard I try. You see, I've never had a sister, and neither has any other man born in space. Not one of us. Never."

Outside the ship the wind was howling now, and they could hear the rattle of sand beating against the metal hull. There was a scraping sound as some desert creature scurried under the ship for shelter against the wind. Tom Barron's face darkened angrily. "I'm not joking," he said. "I'm dead serious. If you're going to sit and laugh we can stop talking right now."

"If you think I'm laughing, you're wrong," Ben said. "All I'm saying is the truth—the only truth there is in this whole fantastic monster story of yours."

"Then what do you mean that you have no sisters?" Tom said.

"I mean just exactly that."

"But why not?"

"Because all the children born to Spacers are male," Ben Trefon said. "In all our history, no Spacer has ever fathered a female child. Boys, yes. Girls, never."

The Barrons stared at each other. "But that doesn't make sense!" Joyce protested. "No people could ever survive without—" She broke off in mid-sentence, her eyes widening.

"You're so right," Ben said. "Without women, we would grow old, and die, and that would be the end of us. And that is the reason why we kidnap women on every raid. There's no other way for us to survive in space."

There was a long silence. Then Joyce shook her head in confusion. "I just don't understand," she said. "How could you possibly have boys but not girls?"

"Because of the gene changes in Spacer men," Ben said. "That part is true, you see. There *are* changes caused by cosmic radiation. The first men in space were damaged, but there were no mutants. The damage was invisible and silent: a tiny change in the cells that reproduce life, actually in just one chromosome pair in those cells, but it was a consistent change that happened every time to every man who came into space. Oh, there were a few other changes. I'm only eighteen, and I'm already graying fast; I'll be white-haired before I'm twenty. And we seem to live a little longer than the average Earthman —our scientists say that our body cells don't age quite as fast, which helps make up for the high death rate from accidents in space. But these are minor things. The change in the sex-determining chromosomes is something else altogether."

"You mean the X-Y pair?"

Ben Trefon nodded. "In Earthmen, women carry a complete pair of chromosomes to determine the sex of the child, while men carry an incomplete pair. One of their X chromosomes is already incomplete—the Y chromosome. When a child is conceived, a combination of an X with an X becomes a female child, while an X and a Y results in a male child."

"Well, anybody knows that," Joyce Barron exclaimed. "That's simple high-school genetics."

"But it's also Earth genetics," Ben said. "In space the single X chromosome that men carry is damaged. Our scientists still don't know how, exactly; some of the genes in the X chromosome are just put out of commission, so that the X behaves like a Y. And as long as Spacer men can provide only Y chromosomes, they can never father girls, only boys."

"Then you mean that all of the women who have been kidnaped from Earth have become Spacer wives?" Tom said.

"Not all of them. No girl has ever been *forced* to become a mauki, and there are always a few who refuse to marry, but not very many. For most of them our life has become their life, and they are as loyal to us as any Spacer man."

"But where do the mutants come from?"

"From your own imagination, nowhere else. There aren't any mutants. Not one. Nowhere. No army of monsters in space getting ready to invade Earth."

Tom Barron was quiet for a long time. Then he said, "But our scientists . . . they actually *saw* mutant children of men who had been in space."

Ben shook his head. "I don't think they did, not really. In the days after the Great War everyone on Earth was bitter, and thousands of lies were told, even by scientists. There must have been some Earthmen who believed that what the Spacers had done was good, and wanted to let them come home. They had to be convinced that exile was the only fate the conspirators deserved. And if people listen to a lie long enough, they come to believe it. Even intelligent, well-trained scientists can have blind spots, as far as the truth is concerned."

Joyce Barron stood up and made some coffee in the galley. The three sat drinking it in silence. Presently the girl said, "If what you are saying is true, you *had* to kidnap women from Earth. It wasn't a matter of choice, but sheer necessity."

"That's right," Ben Trefon said. "We have always held to a rigid quota—only enough women to marry Spacer men as they reached maturity."

"And there never has been an invasion of Earth planned? There's nothing for Earth people to be afraid of?"

"There never has been. There isn't."

"But that would mean that this war, right now, is pointless," Joyce said.

"Pointless and foolish. Based on false premises, on nothing more than ignorance and superstition," Ben said.

"I wish we could believe you," Tom said. "If this is true, it would mean that Joyce has nothing worse to fear than becoming a Spacer's wife."

"That's right," Ben replied. "But it means something else, something that you haven't thought of. You couldn't have thought of it when you boarded the ship, and by now the damage is done."

Tom looked startled. "Damage?"

"If you want to call it that. At least, you've crossed a line since you came aboard. We've been in space a little too long for you to turn back. Whether you like it or not, you're a Spacer now, just like me."

It was not yet dawn when Ben Trefon lifted the little S-80 up into the Martian sky and turned its nose southeast into the sunrise. Below them the desert surface soon became distinct, and Ben began moving the ship close to the surface in a wide zig-zagging path, searching mile upon mile of the surface as it became visible.

"If we move East, we can take advantage of the most sunlight," he said to Tom, who was watching the view screen with him while Joyce prepared the morning meal. "By the time we reach the nightline again, we will have covered all the inhabited part of the planet. There are no houses in the polar regions, and I know the locations of most of the spacer houses and plantations in the temperate and equatorial zones. This way we can find out very quickly what, if anything, is left."

There had been little sleep for any of them that night. For hours through the Martian night they had talked, without embarrassment, without holding back anything. Ben had told them of the Spacers' life, of the great Spacer stronghold at Asteroid Central where the major schools, drydocks, laboratories and factories were to be found, of the nomadic life the Spacers led, of their homes scattered across the solar system, and of the things that they had hoped and dreamed of. And Joyce and Tom had told Ben of their life on Earth's crowded surface, as citizens born and raised on the mother planet.

There had been much to talk about, and it had been a strange conversation, sometimes hot with anger, sometimes confusing, sometimes dazzlingly revealing as they searched for some sort of common ground for understanding. First they needed to find things that they could agree upon. Then they searched out their differing beliefs about each other, the falsehoods and superstitions that had made up the greatest bulk of the things that they "knew" about each other.

It was a frightening and eye-opening conversation for all concerned. Many of the things that were "common knowledge" on Earth about Spacers and their life made Ben's skin crawl, yet he found that there were many things that Spacers "knew" about Earthmen that seemed to fill the Barrons with horror and amazement as well. Ben discovered that his own mental picture of Earth as a vast military garrison-state, with its powerful government police, its injustice, its cruelty and its dictatorial tyranny simply did not jibe with the picture Tom and Joyce drew of their world: a gathering of free nations united in terror and desperation against a frightful threat from the skies, yet a world in which the rights of individuals were jealously guarded, a world in which the everyday life of most of the people was happy, with the same breadth of human emotions and the same concern for human dignity that had always marked the Spacer culture.

As they talked there were many things they flatly did not believe of each other, or would not agree upon. But more and more Ben Trefon had the strange feeling that Tom and Joyce were not lying to him, but actually telling him what they believed. At the same time, he sensed that his own forthright statement of the truth as he knew it was making a deep impression on the two Earth people. It was obviously hard for them to set aside, even momentarily, the beliefs they had held all their lives. Yet Ben was certain that they were puzzled by what he was saying, groping to believe him, trying somehow to fit his viewpoint into their own thoughts and make sense of it.

Above all, the long night's talking revealed a subtle change of attitude on the part of all of them. Much of their earlier hostility was gone, and they no longer listened to each other with flat distrust or disbelief.

Joyce felt free now to ask a question that had been in her mind ever since she first heard the word. "You never really told us," she said to Ben. "What is a mauki? We asked you before, but you didn't say."

"It's so hard to explain," Ben said. "Mauki isn't just a word, and a mauki isn't only a wife and a mother. My father once told me that he wasn't sure but he thought the word itself was a corruption of an old Klickitat Indian word meaning 'warrior who sings.' There is something extra sepcial about a mauki—it has to do with her singing and morale-building. I'm sorry, but this is the best I can do to answer your question, except that I might say without maukis our life would be empty indeed."

"Then," Tom said, "I take it that while all maukis are women, not all women are maukis."

Ben smiled. "Yes, that's right."

Ben would have been furious had anyone a few weeks before suggested that he might actually feel something akin to friendship with any Earthmen, but now he found himself liking this sandy-haired young couple whether he believed what they were saying or not, and could sense their own growing warmth toward him.

As he piloted the little ship on its grim reconnaissance of the ruined planet, he felt a pang of guilt. His companions, technically, were enemy aliens, and their own military forces were responsible for the dreadful wreckage spreading out below them. Yet after their long discussion the night before, Ben realized that he could not properly blame Tom and Joyce Barron for the work of the Earth raiders; he could only stare in heartsick horror at the ruin that ignorance and fear had already spread in its wake.

The Earth ships had done their work well. Hardly a square mile of the inhabited surface of Mars had escaped the furious bombardment. Most of the Spacer houses had been torn to rubble; the few that had been missed had been emptied of their inhabitants, their landing strips and hangars empty. Obviously, some had managed to escape into space before the destruction came. Yet in one place, far out in the desert along the rim of one of the southern rifts the tangled wreckage of a family cruiser, torn to fragments and scattered over a fifty-mile radius, gave mute evidence that even those trying to evacuate had not all escaped.

The dreary search took most of the day. Only once did they discover any sign of life. One of the oldest Spacer houses on Mars had escaped; built deep in the Martian catacombs in the wall of the Great Rift, the House of Wing still stood untouched, and on a second pass over the house Ben saw a small scout ship still snuggled under the protection of overhanging rock. As he dropped down for a landing, he saw a human figure moving out to wave to him.

He landed the ship on null-gravity. The figure was a woman. In one arm she carried an infant; in the other hand was a rifle, held at ready in the crook of her elbow. When Tom started pulling on his pressure suit, Ben shook his head. "Better not," he said. "If she's lost her family, she might lose control. There's nothing you can do out there anyway."

Suited up, Ben dropped down to the rocky landing strip and greeted the mauki by himself. The lines of grief were heavy on her face, but she recognized Ben and remembered traditional Spacer courtesy. Over coffee and crude Martian barley bread she told Ben the story of the raid.

There had been little warning, as Ben had suspected. A fleet of forty Earth ships, of cruiser size, had been detected by Communications at the Experimental Station, but quite naturally had been mistaken for returning Spacer raiders. Before the error was discovered, the ships were already sweeping the planet in pass after pass, unloading air-to-ground missiles in waves. There was no hope of defense; Spacer men had first tried to evacuate their maukis and children, seeking only to break free to the blackness of space, away from the holocaust. A few Spacer ships had mobilized enough to counterattack the bombers on their third pass. There had been a minor skirmish, with a couple of Earth ships shot out of the sky; then the rest of the fleet had drawn back and begun a scattered retreat into space with the few remaining Spacer ships in hot pursuit.

"What kind of ships were they?" Ben had wanted to know.

"Earth ships," the mauki said scornfully. "Slow and crude, clumsily handled. There were just too many, and they came too suddenly. They must have had an orbit ship waiting for them out there somewhere; with ion drive, those ships could never have come straight from Earth by themselves."

"Any word back from our own ships?"

The mauki shook her head sadly. "Nothing. The Earthmen hit and ran, moved out when their dirty work was done. Then after it was all over, the survivors here went on, in whatever ships were still spaceworthy."

"What about you?" Ben asked gently.

"Someone had to stay, to pass the word to our own raiders coming back. There was no reason for me to go. My man was killed trying to reach the family ship, along with the two older boys. Why should I go now?"

"Then what are the orders?"

The woman shook her head, "No orders, just a vague plan. The men wanted to get to Asteroid Central as soon as they could; there's bound to be murder out in the rings. They figured that some of our spies on Earth must have been broken somehow, or else we had traitors in our midst. How else could they have hit every house here, every farm? But in space, they can't fight us. If enough ships can get to Central soon enough, they may be able to stop an attack there."

Ben thought it over, frowning. "Maybe," he said. "But if all our ships start converging on Asteroid Central, wouldn't that be painting it red for the enemy?"

"The men thought of that. They won't be going directly to Central. Each one picked one of the outpost asteroids. They were hoping to draw the Earth fleet into a booby trap, thinking it was Asteroid Central, and then hit both flanks. Nobody seemed to think the Earth fleet could hold up for an hour in a real space attack."

"I'm not so sure," Ben said, thinking of the driving fear that the Barrons had spoken of. "They might try to fight their way through to Central no matter what their losses. How long ago did the last ship leave?"

"Twenty-four hours ago. The plan was for any of the raiders returning to head for Asteroid Central, and join forces with any major Spacer ship they could contact."

"Then I'll have to move," Ben said. "Do you have food and water, enough for you and the baby?"

"We have plenty," the woman said. "And we have fuel stores. You'd better load all you can carry."

For the next half-hour Ben loaded the lead-shielded fuel blocks into the ship's hold, discarding the exhausted stores. Normally these would be picked up by a "scavenger" ship, carried to a roving tanker plying its route out to the asteroid rings, and ultimately reach the great nuclear fuel repositories in the breeder piles on Asteroid Central, for refilling. But now, he reflected, there was no telling when the empties would be refilled.

Once again aboard the ship, after a few words of encouragement to the desolated mauki, Ben activated the null-gravs and moved up into the thin Martian atmosphere. As briefly as he could, and without going into detail, he told the Barrons their destination: a swift trip out from the orbit of Mars into the barren "desert" of the asteroid rings, with sights set on a rendezvous and regrouping with Spacer forces somewhere in the vicinity of Asteroid Central. "There's no choice but to take you along," he told them. "You'd not be safe on Mars, not with her."

"How many people escaped?" Joyce Barron asked.

"Only a handful. Probably ninety per cent of the people were destroyed in their houses."

"It's terrible," Joyce said, "without any warning, and no quarter given to women and children. If that many were killed spread out all over a planet, think what could happen to your central city in the Rings. . . ."

Ben Trefon gave her a long look. "It's terrible to think about, all right," he said. "But I think you've got it backwards."

"Backwards?"

"Mars was one thing. Asteroid Central is something else

altogether. On Mars it was your kind of war on the surface of a planet with a thick blanket of atmosphere. This round has gone to you, but when you stir up a nest of hornets, you'd better be able to run. In battle in open space your ships won't stand a chance of beating us. You'll be wiped out of the sky."

Tom Barron looked skeptical. "Maybe," he said.

"You don't believe me?"

"I think I would, except for one thing that you aren't considering," Tom said. "Remember that your own ships are fighting to stay alive. Ours aren't. As far as they know, the men in our fleet believe they are already contaminated beyond help by radiation. They have no hope of ever coming home again. And that means that your men are going to be fighting a suicide fleet." Tom looked up at Ben Trefon. "They may not be so easy to wipe out of the sky as you think."

With the rusty disk of Mars far behind them and the sun a small gleaming beacon in the blackness, the two Earth prisoners and their Spacer captor set their ship's course for the long pull outward toward the Rings.

If the ruined houses and plantations on Mars were Spacer outposts in the solar system, the asteroid belt was their heartland, the vast and mysterious spaces where only Spacers were equipped to survive. With the nose of the ship pointed away from the sun, Ben Trefon began plotting their course, his heart growing lighter by the minute.

It was true, of course, that the first battle of this war had gone to the Earthmen. It might also be true that the pilots of the Earth fleet would be desperate men, ready to fight to the bitter end in their quest to stamp out every vestige of Spacer culture in the solar system. But every Spacer knew that nature had no feelings or emotions, no respect for human valiance, or courage, or even desperation. Any ships in space, no matter how determined their crews, would face the cold equations of celestial physics; the prize would go to the experienced and skillful, not to the brave or the desperate. And this meant that no fleet of Earth ships could hope to excel the long training and familiarity with space, the enormous skill in navigation and space maneuver that the Spacers possessed.

The Spacers' major problem would be mobilization of their forces into an effective force to oppose the Earth fleet, and then to drive it into battle in the depths of space. This would take organization and planning. In the meantime, Ben thought coldly, the more confident the Earthmen became, the harder their fall when the awakening came. The annihilation on Mars was dreadful, but it was also futile, for it would be repaid a thousand times over in the great empty spaces of the asteroids.

For Ben, the problem now was to reach the vicinity of Asteroid Central without encounter with any of the Earth fleet, and then establish contact with the Spacer command trying to organize defending forces. He knew that the great Spacer stronghold was in opposition to Mars at this time of year, so that the course was outward from Mars's orbit to that of the asteroid. A few moments' work with the computer set the basic course. As the Barrons watched the panorama of stars through the view screen Ben settled down to the job of calculating a fast, precise route of approach.

His prisoners seemed fascinated by the panoply of stars, far more numerous than those visible through Earth's atmosphere blanket, and by the sun which appeared much smaller here than on Earth. But something else seemed to be puzzling them as the ship's course was set and acceleration began. They seemed to be searching the blackness, looking for something.

"What's the matter?" Ben said. "What are you looking for?"

"The Rings, of course," Tom Barron said.

"We've been in the Rings for three hours," Ben said. "Ever since we left Mars. We're approaching the first concentration ring of asteroids in another hour or so."

"Then where are the asteroids?" Tom wanted to know.

Ben grinned and scratched his jaw. "Well, let's take a look." He whirled the dial of the radar scanner through all quadrants, watching for the characteristic light spot that would signal one of the flecks of interplanetary debris. From time to time in the view screen the Barrons could see brief flickers of light, almost like lightning, around the ship. "Of course, those are asteroids too," Ben said, "dust-particle size, or sand-grain size. The ship has a force screen to atomize them as we go; if it didn't they'd just punch holes through one side of the ship and out the other as well as through anybody that happened to be in the way. But let's find you a big one."

After ten minutes of scanning, a characteristic blip appeared on the radar screen in the segment of space they were approaching. On the tracking screen a red line appeared, showing the gentle arc the contacted object was following in relation to the ship's course since the moment of contact. Ben uncapped the eyepieces of the co-ordinated telescope, picked up the object itself outlined in the eerie shadow of the distant sun. As it came closer, it resolved into a solid-appearing mass, and Ben moved aside so that the Barrons could peer through the 'scope.

The asteroid was a ragged, irregular chunk of rock, perhaps forty feet in diameter, rolling crazily end-over-end as it moved in its orbit. Small as it was, it carried with it a fuzzy halo of reflected light around it, the collection of satellite asteroid particles that accompanied it in its course around the sun. As the Barrons watched, Ben adjusted the course a fraction of a degree to stay clear of the rock, until it had passed and vanished from the range of the telescope.

Ben laughed at Tom's crestfallen expression as he recapped the eyepieces. "Not very impressive, eh?"

"Not only that," Tom said. "You had to hunt so long for it. I thought the Asteroid Belt was full of them."

"It is, compared to the rest of interplanetary space," Ben said. "There are millions and millions of those little rocks floating around the sun with their orbits in this general area. But there's also a whale of a lot of space between the orbits of Mars and Jupiter for the asteroids to fill. There's so much space that a ship moving through the Rings rarely encounters anything much larger than a sand grain, unless he goes looking for it. You'll only find one rock of significant size in every four hundred square miles in the plane we're moving in, and you'd have to search about thirty-five thousand square miles to find a rock big enough to make a landing on."

Tom had been watching the radar screen as they talked. Now he scratched his head. "Maybe so," he said. "But then you're beating the statistics already. Look at that."

Another blip had appeared on the radar screen. The contact lay off the starboard bow of the ship, at the outer limits of the radar's range. As they watched a bright red line began to appear again on the tracking screen.

Ben crossed the hairlines on the tracking screen, punched a stopwatch, recrossed them ten seconds later, and frowned. "Sure looks like another rock," he said. "And a big one, too. Pretty close to collision course with us." He punched figures into the computer, adjusted the ship's course a hair. "This one should be easy to pick up with the 'scope."

He swung the 'scope into co-ordination with the radar beam and peered through the eyepiece. For a moment he just sat looking, moving the 'scope controls from time to time. "Hm," he said finally. "Something's out of whack here."

"What's the matter?" Tom Barron wanted to know.

"I'm not sure. I can't pick it up in the 'scope. But look at the tracing screen."

The red line had begun to curve. A moment before it had been approaching Ben's ship in a straight 45-degree trajectory;

now it was curving upward on the screen until it was almost parallel to the white line of the little S-80.

Tom Barron looked up at Ben. "Since when can an asteroid change course?"

"It can't," Ben said. "That's no asteroid. "That's a ship under power. And it's close enough for us to see it." He turned back to the telescope, searching the area of space where the intruding ship had to be. He went back and searched again, more carefully, with growing alarm. The ship, or whatever it was, was unquestionably close enough for reflected light to reveal it as Ben crisscrossed the area a third time.

But there was no image of any kind in the telescope.

Tom Barron started to say something, but Ben waved him to silence. There was something wrong here, something Ben simply couldn't understand. Friend or foe, there was a ship out there, probably no more than fifty linear miles from his own ship, moving on a parallel course with his ship. The tracking screen showed it to be moving at precisely the same speed. The radar said plainly that it was there . . . but the telescope revealed no sign of it.

And that, of course, was flatly impossible. Any ship or any other object in space that would show up on a short-range radar scanner should be equally visible in the telescope. With the new intensifiers to quadruple the light-gathering power of the telescope's lenses, even a ship deliberately painted flat black to reduce its reflectivity should stand out like a beacon in the sky. But this area of space appeared utterly empty.

Thoroughly alarmed now, Ben turned back to the ship's controls. He had encountered his share of curious happenings in space, but this was something new. "Tom, you'd better strap down here and keep an eye on the tracing screen for me. Joyce, you get secured on a cot. We're going to do some jumping around."

Very slightly, Ben dropped the ship's acceleration, and shifted its course away from the mysterious intruder. Without a moment's hesitation, the red line on the screen also slowed and veered. Ben veered more sharply, this time in toward the intruder in a long flat arc. The red line veered instantly to match the move again. Whatever it was, it had attached itself to the little S-80 and was following its maneuvers move by move with rather amazing agility. Once more Ben tried to telescope, with no more success than before.

"Look, what's going on?" Tom Barron demanded.

"I don't know," Ben said. "But whatever it is, I don't like

it. There's something out there that behaves like a ship, but I can't pick it up on the 'scope."

"Maybe it has some kind of masking device," Tom said.

Ben looked up at him sharply. "We've been trying to develop a masking device for ships for decades, and we haven't gotten to first base. Unless your people have stumbled onto one that we've never heard of."

Tom looked dubious. "If we had, seems to me we would have been using it for ground protection during raids."

"Exactly," Ben said. Once again he veered the S-80 in toward the intruder, watched the red line veer away in tandem. "They don't want to close in on us, they're just staying on our tail." He peered through the view screen at the empty expanse of space, saw the flat brilliance of the sun's disk and the thin red fingernail of Mars now visible at the extreme edge of the screen. "And they don't want to be seen . . . well, maybe we can chisel a look all the same. Hold on."

With a few swift moves Ben activated the ship's side jets, and began a sharp banking maneuver, turning the ship as hard as he could. In the engine room the null-grav generators whined in protest at the overload; Ben eased up momentarily, then banked again, turning the ship through a 180-degree arc in a series of sharp maneuvers. With each shift the red line on the tracer screen followed suit, shifting and straightening. Ben's little ship bucked and shuddered under the impact of force vectors it was never expected to withstand, and his passengers gripped their shock bars for dear life.

But in the space of a few moments he had turned the ship in a full half-circle, so that the sun's bright disk lay full in the view screen with the intruder moving somewhere between him and the sun.

A few more carefully calculated moves did it. The tracer screen was three-dimensional, with co-ordinates zeroed in the plane of the sun's orbit. Now Ben calculated his ship's angle in relation to the sun's plane, and figured the intruder's angle as well. Abruptly, Ben dipped the little ship's nose down so that the intruder lay in a straight line between the S-80 and the sun.

An instant later the phantom ship seemed to recognize Ben's trap; the red line veered downward sharply. But it was already too late. For the space of a few seconds the sun's disk was blotted out, eclipsed by the phantom. Prepared and waiting, Ben punched a stopwatch. Moments later the shadow was gone, and Ben stopped the timer. "Got him," he said. "Tom, read that interval dial."

Tom read the figures on the tracing screen indicating the phantom ship's distance from their own ship at the instant its hulk had crossed in front of the sun. Swiftly Ben taped the figures into the computer, adding the ship's velocity and the length of the eclipse. It was crude calculation, ignoring a couple of minor variables, but it would be close enough to tell Ben what he wanted to know. The computer buzzed for a moment, and ejected a card.

Ben looked at it, and sucked his breath in between his teeth.

There was something out there, all right. Almost beyond doubt, it was a ship . . . a phantom ship that could somehow mask itself from observation by reflected light. But it was made of solid matter that could not avoid masking the sun's disk as it passed between the sun and the observer.

And it was no ordinary space ship. The answer on the card was hardly believable; the ship was huge, larger than any Spacer cruiser, larger than the largest orbit ship the Spacers had ever built. It was a ship so large that it defied belief, and yet it was there.

What was more, the phantom ship must have realized what Ben Trefon had done, for a moment later it suddenly veered away from the parallel course it had been following and moved swiftly out into the darkness of the asteroid Rings. Within a few seconds it disappeared from the radar scanner, as though once detected it no longer dared to stay.

As suddenly as it had appeared, it was gone. But much as he tried to conceal his alarm from his prisoners, Ben Trefon could not conceal it from himself. The Barrons might assume that it had merely been another Spacer ship making a reconnaissance run without stopping for contact, but Ben could not brush the incident aside so easily.

He was reasonably certain that the phantom was not a Spacer ship. But that was not what worried him. The real trouble was that he was equally certain that it was no ship that had ever been built on Earth either.

6 THE FACE OF THE ENEMY

IN THE FIRST few minutes after the mysterious intruder vanished, Ben had plenty of routine navigational work to do to keep his mind off the strange encounter. The course of the little S-80 had to be rectified and a new course plotted, since the maneuverings had involved both movement through space and loss of time on the previous plotting. But the work was largely automatic once the computations were complete; Ben's hands went through the motions as his mind worked feverishly to make some sense out of the phantom ship and the things its visit implied.

The truth was that the encounter had shaken him up badly. Tom and Joyce Barron appeared to have shrugged the incident off without much concern and began busying themselves among the ship's music tapes. It seemed obvious that the real significance of the encounter simply had not dawned on them.

Which was just as well for the moment, Ben thought wryly. It kept them from asking him a lot of unanswerable questions, and gave him time to search out some answers for himself . . . answers that had to be found and found quickly. With the ship's course returned to its original direction, Ben sat back at the controls, trying to push confusion and bafflement out of his mind and make sense out of nonsense.

Certain things, he knew, were beyond argument. The ship had been there. Nothing but a manned craft could have behaved the way the phantom had behaved. Crude as his computations had been, he was certain that they had given him at least a rough estimate of its size. And there was no question but that it had been concealed most effectively from observation. These were things he would testify to. But put them together and they spelled nothing but nonsense.

There simply could not be any such ship. He knew, of course, that the Spacer military council did not make public all the weapons in the arsenal on Asteroid Central, but Spacers were too small and close-knit a group for secrets to keep long. The discovery of null-gravity had been common knowledge among Spacers before the first prototype engine had been completed. Whenever new defensive missiles had been developed, the whole Spacer clan knew about them in a matter of weeks. And even if the phantom *had* been a Spacer ship developed in secrecy, it surely would have recognized the S-80 as a Spacer ship and at least exchanged recognition signals.

But the other alternative—that it was an Earth ship—was even more ridiculous. Suppose Earth science could have developed such a craft, what could explain its strange behavior after contact? It too would have been able to recognize a Spacer scout. Then why had Ben's ship not been attacked? Even if a crew of Earthmen aboard had known of Ben's prisoners, they certainly would have made an effort to grapple his ship and unload his hostages. And for that matter, where could Earthmen have learned such skill in maneuvering, especially in maneuvering such a huge ship?

Either way it made no sense, and it was this very senselessness that sent a cold chill up Ben Trefon's back and brought sweat out on the palms of his hands. The phantom ship had not behaved like an aggressor, or like a friend either. Its behavior had seemed more curious than warlike, as though it had been trying to observe him without being observed, and then had zoomed off again as soon as it knew it was detected.

But zoomed off to where? That, of course, was the big question. If the intruder had been curious, perhaps he was still curious enough to follow Ben's ship from some point beyond effective radar range. That in itself was a disquieting thought. If Ben were to pursue his original plans to reach one of the outpost asteroids near Asteroid Central he did not care to bring unexpected company with him.

Carefully, he turned other possibilities over in his mind. He could, of course, change course and make his way directly to Asteroid Central. And if his encounter had been with an orthodox ship, he might well have done that. He knew the kind of ingenious fortification that surrounded Asteroid Central; prior to his encounter with the phantom ship he had been supremely confident that no enemy ship could follow him through the Maze to the surface of Central and survive, no matter how hard they tried. But *this* ship might be a different kind of pursuer altogether, a pursuer with totally unexpected capabilities in space.

Ben scratched his jaw and glanced back at the Barrons who were now entranced by some tapes of mauki songs. Whatever else it did, the encounter changed his mind about trying to go it alone to Asteroid Central. For a moment he seemed to hear his father's voice in his ear: "Never insist on doing it alone if you can't handle it. Admit your limitations and don't be ashamed to get help. Remember, a whole army of men have died in space just because they were too stiff-necked to ask for help, or too stupid to tell when they needed it in the first place."

Ben was certain now that he needed help, needed it badly enough to take chances to get it. Other Spacer ships would be converging on Outpost 5, his immediate target destination, a medium-sized asteroid moving in its orbit some two hundred thousand miles in from Asteroid Central. Outpost 5 was a Spacer utility station: a fuel and ammunition dump, orbit-ship drydock, laying-over station for Spacers in transit and repair station for the Spacer fleet. Ben had originally intended to move into contact with Outpost 5 as silently as possible. Now it was imperative that he establish contact with other Spacer ships before the outpost was reached.

This meant breaking radio silence in order to flag the attention of other ships which might be in the same segment of space. A risky business, for Earth ships also would be traveling in this sector, but at least Earth ships could be understood and dealt with.

And Ben Trefon was not at all too certain about the phantom ship he had encountered.

He made contact with another Spacer some six hours later, as the little S-80 moved closer and closer to contact orbit with the Outpost 5 asteroid.

With every passing hour Ben's tension had been growing. He had not dared to throw open his radio with a standard distress signal. Instead, he had beamed out five-minute periods of signaling, trying to cover all quadrants briefly with a signal that would be identifiable to any Spacer craft without continuing long enough for an enemy ship to fix his position and acceleration in space. After each signal period he had waited, straining to catch even the weakest response signal. It had been a long and weary vigil. Over eighteen hours had passed since the sleep period on Mars, and the Barrons had finally grown bored and retired; Ben's body ached with fatigue, and he longed for a few moments' rest, but knew that those few moments could lose him his chance for contact.

So he stuck it out in the silence of the little ship's cabin. The view screen showed an unchanging panorama of pinpoint stars on a velvet black canopy; Ben felt utterly alone and abandoned as his repeated efforts to raise a friendly signal failed.

Then, unexpectedly, there was a tiny blip on the radar scanner. As he drew closer the blip resolved into two, and then into a dozen. With the telescope he scanned the area of the contact, and decelerated the ship as rapidly as the null-gravs would permit. Moments later he saw the objects his radar had picked up, and drew in his breath sharply.

It was no wonder there had been no radio response from Outpost 5.

He had wandered into a cosmic battlefield. Far and wide over a four-hundred-mile radius the debris of shattered space ships was spread. A great Spacer cruiser was reeling end-over-end, its side split open like a pea-pod with bits and pieces strewn around it like a halo. Looking more closely, he spotted an Earth ship, also of cruiser size, literally torn into shreds. Fragments of other ships, fuel tanks, oxygen bottles and bombarded lifeboats came into view as he approached. At least half a dozen ships had been involved in the battle. Now there was no sign of life anywhere in the vicinity .

But a demand signal from Ben's transmitter brought a feeble response. Scanning the area again, Ben saw another Spacer ship well beyond the debris-scattered area. It was a small, three-man ship, one of the SD-7's that Spacers so often used as family craft, and it was under power in spite of the gaping hole torn in the engine-room hull and the drunken roll that signified that its stabilizing gyros were no longer functioning properly. As Ben moved closer, he recognized the brilliant black-and-white decoration and insignia of a ship that he had seen many times in the hangar of the House of Trefon. It was the ship owned by Roger Petro, one of the men in the Spacer Council and one of Ivan Trefon's closest friends.

Now the response to Ben's signal was stronger as he moved into orbit alongside the Spacer ship. He could see movement on the hull; two or three men were working there with welding torches, obviously trying to repair the hole in the ship's skin. Locking his ship's controls in parallel with the SD-7, Ben checked to be certain the Barrons were still sleeping. Then he donned a pressure suit, climbed aboard the little scooter that served as the S-80's lifeboat, and piloted himself across the intervening space to Petro's ship.

The men on the hull greeted him with waves. Moments later he was aboard to find Petro himself in a bunk in the ship's cabin, one arm in a sling, and one leg splinted and wrapped with a red-stained bandage. Petro looked pale and haggard, but his eyes lit up when he saw his visitor.

"Come in, boy!" he bellowed. "This old crate hasn't much

to offer right now, but I guess Ivan Trefon's boy won't mind greeting an old soldier on the battlefield, eh?"

"What happened?" Ben wanted to know.

"Get yourself some coffee, boy, and sit down; let me look at you."

Ben poured a cup of vile-looking black stuff. It was as strong as it looked. "What happened?" he repeated.

"I caught one broadside, that's what happened," Petro said. "Too many of them and too few of us, at first. We ran into a nest of them heading out toward Outpost 5, and they buried me in fire power. Too many shells to stop too quickly. Seven of them blasting away at the same time."

"Seven! How many got away?"

Petro chuckled. "You should have counted the nose cones on the way in," he said. "Any time old Petro can't handle seven Earth ships at a time and bring them to heel, it'll be time he turns his ship over to a better man."

"Any survivors?"

"That's why we're standing by, to make sure there aren't any," Petro said. "Treacherous dogs! One of them actually rode a shell right into this ship. Used a hand gun to detonate our defense shells. He hit us right in the guts, and blooey!" The Spacer shook his head. "Of course he didn't know where to aim, so all he did was to get our stabilizing gyros. Except for that we'd have gotten to Outpost 5 already. But enough of this—how are things on Mars?"

Ben told him how things were on Mars. Petro sat silent, clenching his fist as he heard about the raid, the ruin of the House of Trefon and the loss of his old friend. "I knew I should have headed there first after the raid," he muttered finally. "And I was afraid there was trouble when there was no word from Mars on any of the ships I've contacted out here."

"You mean *none* got completely away?" Ben said.

"I mean I haven't been in touch with any." The old man crashed his fist down on the bunk bitterly. "The treacherous dogs! They know where Asteroid Central is, all right, and this part of the Rings is full of them, regular nests of them. But they won't hit us openly, out in space where we can fight them! They hide until they find one of us alone—" He broke off with a sigh. "At least a couple were stupid enough to try to run the Maze into Asteroid Central itself, but now I've heard they've pulled back and started sniping."

"But where are our own ships?"

"Mostly back at Central. Then, as far as I've heard, all the outpost stations are manned; four were attacked and held off the enemy without half trying. I was on my way to check in at Outpost 5 and try to organize a drive to break the siege at Asteroid Central."

Ben nodded. "We were headed for 5 too." He hesitated. "Have you seen anything funny out here, except standard Earth ships?"

Petro looked up at him sharply. His leg was obviously paining him; for a moment he set his teeth until the spasm eased up. "What do you mean, anything funny?"

"Well . . . anything that didn't seem right to you," Ben said.

Petro shrugged. "Nothing much. We had a false contact a day or so back, but nothing we could pin down."

"You mean a ship you couldn't identify?"

"Thought it was a ship, but it couldn't have been. The radar picked up something for a couple of minutes, but we couldn't see it in the 'scope, and then it was gone."

"But it was close enough so that your 'scope should have picked it up," Ben said.

Petro chewed his lip for a moment. "What are you getting at, boy?"

Ben hesitated. Faced with the keen eyes and the long experience of the old Spacer, he realized how foolish the story of a giant invisible ship would sound. But it had been there, whether Petro chose to believe him or not. Ben told the councilman about his own encounter, and the maneuver that allowed him to see the ship and take a gross measurement. He expected a guffaw from the old soldier, but Petro didn't even smile. "It's happened before," he said. "Usually been chalked up to too much red-eye and a bored pilot, but there's never been a report of anyone actually *seeing* it."

"It was there," Ben said. "I saw it."

"But these reports were long before this blow-up started," Petro said.

"Maybe they've had a spy ship out here that we haven't known about. They knew the location of every house on Mars; they didn't waste any shells."

They talked it over for a few more moments, but neither of them came up with any answer. Finally Ben said, "What are you planning now?"

"I'm going to limp on out to Outpost 5, if the boys ever get the gyros fixed. Most of the Earth ships are clustered around Asteroid Central, maybe five hundred of them, trying to figure out a way to get ships or shells through the Maze.

And that's fine for now, but Central can't stand a prolonged siege. Sooner or later they'll get a shell through by sheer chance; we've got to break them apart before they do it. And they're out to annihilate every Spacer alive, man, woman and child."

"Why travel with this ship?" Ben said. "You and your crew could come aboard with me."

Petro shook his head. "No, I don't think so. As long as this ship still has power, I'll stay aboard her."

"Suppose you run across another crowd of Earth ships?"

The old Spacer shrugged. "We're going to run across a lot of Earth ships before this war is over," he said slowly. "Your father didn't have a chance to fight. I've got fighting to do for both of us, and I'm going to do it in my own ship."

"Then at least team up with me," Ben Trefon said. "I can hold my own in a fight."

For a moment Petro looked him over. Then he chuckled. "Yes, I think you probably can. But you said you had a couple of captives. What about them?"

"There's nothing they can do. In fact, this jaunt has been an eye-opener for them. They aren't so sure that this war even makes sense any more."

Petro grunted. "That's all very well, but don't trust them. Don't trust them for a minute. Earthmen are Earthmen, and you can't change that overnight."

Quickly then they made plans. Petro would follow Ben's course on toward Outpost 5; in the event of an encounter, they would work as a combat team. Because of Ben's greater maneuverability until Petro got his ship to drydock, it was decided that Ben should assume command. With the details agreed upon, Ben donned his pressure suit again. The firm pressure of the black web belt around his waist reminded him of a final question. "Do you happen to remember a black belt that Dad used to wear?" he asked Petro.

"A web belt with a capsule in it?" Petro nodded. "Some kind of a keepsake, wasn't it?"

"I guess so," Ben said. "Did Dad ever say anything about it to you?"

"Not that I can remember." Petro frowned. "Though it seems to me he once said he wanted you to have it when he died. Didn't you find it on Mars?"

"Oh, I found it, all right," Ben replied. "But it's an odd kind of belt."

Petro shrugged. "Your father seemed to like it. Said it might bring him good luck, and you too. Maybe it will. I've a hunch you're going to need it."

And on that, at least, Ben Trefon was ready to agree.

The next few hours were tense as the two ships began accelerating together toward the rendezvous point with Outpost 5 asteroid, Ben Trefon's little S-80 in the lead, followed closely by the crippled cruiser manned by Petro's crew. The ships kept close contact by means of tight-beam transmitter in order to minimize the chances of ships beyond them picking up the signals. Working together, they set the course that would intersect the orbit of the outpost at the precise point in space and time necessary for contact.

And then they sat back and waited.

They knew, of course, that the course would not be a hundred per cent accurate, no matter how carefully it was plotted. Precise as their calculations were, they could not take into account every one of the minor variables in an asteroid's orbit. Theoretically it was possible to calculate such an orbit down to inches for any given instant in time; but on board a ship it just wasn't practical. Asteroids followed elliptical orbits around the sun, just like all other planetary bodies, and their speed in orbit varied from moment to moment, gradually increasing as they moved in toward perihelion and slowing down bit by bit as they moved out toward aphelion. In addition, the asteroids affected each other's orbital velocities slightly, exerting weak but significant gravitational attraction for one another as they passed. Finally there was mighty Jupiter to take into account; in the Asteroid Belt, Jupiter was king, its powerful gravitational field pulling and tugging at the asteroids in its titanic effort to bring them under control.

Astronomers had their pet theories. Some insisted that at some time in the distant future mighty Jupiter would win the struggle and ultimately capture many of the asteroidal fragments. Others would destroy themselves in collisions with each other and still others would be kept from wandering by gravitational forces until each asteroid had a completely predictable orbit. But other scientists insisted that the turbulence of movement in the Asteroid Belt would never cease; that any effort to pinpoint exactly where a given asteroid was going to be at a given time would be doomed to failure to the end of time.

These things did not disturb Ben Trefon. Space navigators had long since discovered that their targets were never precisely where they were supposed to be, no matter how fine the course was calculated. Ben knew that he would have to rely upon visual sighting, radar contact and radio guideposts when he reached the near vicinity of the outpost. But outpost asteroids were well equipped with powerful transmitters to guide in any approaching Spacer ship.

After Ben returned from Petro's ship, he found the Barrons burning with curiosity. Ben set the course and started acceleration; then he reviewed for them what he and Petro had discussed. He told them about Petro's encounter with the Earth ships, and the outline of the plan they were following.

Tom Barron's forehead creased with worry. "I don't understand," he said. "If our ships have actually located your Asteroid Central, then you must be under attack there right now. Why aren't you going there?"

"Because we need organization first," Ben said. "Anyway, there's no way Earth ships can be attacking, even if they're on all sides of Central. That's what the Maze is there for."

"What maze?" Tom Barron said.

"The maze of asteroids surrounding Asteroid Central," Ben said. "When Earth started sending out pirates against us a century or so ago, our Council realized that a couple of well-placed nuclear bombs could blow Central to pieces, so they built a maze of small rocks around Central to detonate any shells that might strike home. Quite a feat of planetary engineering, hauling in mile-wide rocks and launching them in orbit around Central with Central as the primary. But now Central is surrounded by a regular swarm of satellites, moving in all directions and angles, at a dozen or more rates of speed. Any ship that tries to approach Central now without knowing the safe navigation key doesn't stand a chance in three billion of actually reaching target. It would have fifteen or twenty collisions with smaller asteroids first, and when a space ship collides with an asteroid, believe me, the asteroid wins."

Tom thought that over. "How many asteroids are there in the Maze?"

"About three thousand, spread out in a hundred-mile radius."

"But how do *you* get through it?"

"Well, we know the safe navigation key, for one thing. It's taped into our ships' computers. Even so it's a tricky navigational problem, since the key is never one hundred per cent right. We have to know how to handle our ships. In fact, approach to Asteroid Central is required navigation training for any Spacer who wants to operate a ship, sort of a graduation exercise. As for a ship that doesn't know the key, or one with a poor navigator, the Maze is doubly treacherous. It's a one-way road; once a ship starts in, it's certain death to try to back out again, and just as deadly to try to sit still. Once you start in, you keep going or you get smashed. It doesn't pay to get cold feet halfway through."

Tom was still puzzled. "And you mean to say you went to all that trouble just because of the patrol ships we sent up?"

"What else could we do if one ship could carry one bomb that would split Central into fragments if it were launched without warning?"

Joyce, who had been following the conversation silently, joined in now. "I just can't believe that an Earth captain would fire on a city without warning," she said.

"Mars didn't get much warning," Ben said.

"But that was in war."

"Do you think we were at peace before?" Ben asked. "Did you ever hear the things your pirate ships did when they came out here looking for us?"

Joyce shook her head. "Just that they'd recovered food stores that had been stolen. Of course, before we had radiation shielding on our ships, those crews had to be interned for months, and sometimes reports were slow."

Ben nodded grimly. "And incomplete, I'll bet. You never heard about the time Outpost 7 was bombed to rubble a few years ago, women, children, and all? They never told you about the maukis that were kidnaped? About the two-year-old baby they took back to Earth and kept in a completely black room for fourteen years without contact with another human being? Or about the children they jettisoned into space through the rocket tubes without space suits?"

Tom and Joyce Barron just stared at him. "There never were any such stories."

"I don't imagine there were," Ben said bitterly. "Don't you see that you've only been told what your government wanted you to know? But the truth is the truth. Your expeditionary ships would murder every Spacer child they came across; there was no limit to the torment they spread before they could be driven back. We knew we couldn't barricade all space, but maybe you can understand why we barricaded Asteroid Central with the Maze."

Under their feet they could feel the throbbing hum of the null-gravity generators; on the control panel the computer clucked occasionally like a worried hen, and the radio beam to Petro's ship chattered its contact signal at periodic intervals.

The Barrons were silent for a moment, and Ben realized that once again they were at loggerheads; they could not believe him, yet neither could they believe that he was lying to them. Finally Joyce Barron sighed. "You make us sound beastly," she said. "But you just ignore our side of the picture. You don't pay any attention to how *we* felt, never knowing when another raid would come. You don't understand how our people dreaded those raids, knowing they were coming and knowing that sisters or daughters would be stolen away and disappear forever. And you don't say anything about the murder and mayhem your own raiders were responsible for on Earth."

Ben nodded. "I know people were killed in the raids," he said. "But it was never murder for the sake of murder. And that was why we developed the tangle-guns, so we could defend ourselves on Earth raids without hurting people. As for the kidnapings, if Earth had let us come down in peace to find our wives, there wouldn't have been any kidnapings, and no kidnaped girl was every forced into marriage against her will. None of the girls liked the idea at first, but when they heard the songs and stories and saw the way we lived—" He spread his hands. "You would have to look far and wide today to find a disloyal mauki."

The conversation lagged as Ben corrected course and then broke radio silence to check with Petro. The periodic recognition signal beamed ahead toward Outpost 5 still failed to raise a response, even though the two ships were now approaching rendezvous point very rapidly.

"Any sign of life?" Petro asked in the earphones.

"Not a peep. I wonder what's wrong?"

"They're probably afraid to break silence until we're close enough for a tight beam to hit us without hitting a dozen Earth ships too."

"But we're already close enough for that," Ben protested.

"Well, keep trying. And don't get nervous. The boys on 5 know what's up there better than we do. If they think a signal will draw a wolf pack, they may make us home in without a signal."

Ben kept trying, but he couldn't hide his growing apprehension. With the ship now decelerating again, he watched the dials turn as the distance to contact point diminished. Tom and Joyce watched the radar screen over his shoulder. A half hour passed, and then another, with no answer to Ben's signal.

Then the radar screen picked up a response, the faintest suggestion of a blip where Outpost 5 should be located. Excitedly, Ben activated the tracking screen, superimposed the calculated orbit of Outpost 5 on the same screen, and saw that they coincided exactly. He tapped the signal button to Petro's ship. "We're there," he said. "I should have a sighting in a minute."

"Well, hang onto it," Petro said. "I just had another generator go. I haven't even got radar."

"Then stick close. I'll guide you in."

After the hours of tension, the contact was an almost unbelievable relief. Jubilantly Ben tightened down his signal arc and beamed his recognition signal toward the outpost. After the long hours of going it alone, here was a safe haven, a port in this storm of space invaders, a place to rest and contact other Spacers and make plans to fight back the foe that was threatening their very existence. Until now Ben had not realized how much alone and helpless he had felt since his first look at the ruined House of Trefon. Now at least he would have an effective way to fight back.

Suddenly the outpost asteroid appeared in the telescope, growing from a flicker of light to a distinct disk as they approached. But once again Ben saw the ship's guard screens flaring as bits of rubble and debris floating in space were contacted. The rubble thickened, and some of the larger fragments became visible as they drew nearer the asteroid.

Outpost 5 had not escaped attack, after all. There had been a battle here, probably only a few hours before, judging from the density of the debris. Ben strained for an answering signal from the outpost but still there was no response. Something stirred in his mind as he stared at the asteroid. He could make out some of the surface detail now. The outpost had an empty, abandoned look about it. There were no surrounding Spacer ships, no signs of life. He beamed his signal again, waiting uneasily for an answer. By now there should have been a response; the powerful transmitters on the outpost could not have been destroyed completely, and his ship was close enough for clear recognition.

After a moment's hesitation Ben rapped out the Spacer's distress signal, an imperative demand for response. For a long moment there was silence. Then, feebly, a response came back on a tight beam. But it was not an identification signal. It was an SOS, repeated over and over as though being transmitted by tape in a feeble stream from the outpost radios.

Ben signaled Petro. "Are you getting that?" he asked.

"Yes," Petro said. "They're in trouble."

"I can't get an ID from them.' '

"That's an automatic response," Petro replied. "And look at that rock! They must have taken a pounding."

It was true. As they moved closer Ben could see the pockmarks and craters in the surface of the rock, telltale evidence of a terrific bombardment. Now Ben could see that the asteroid was listing and wobbling slightly as it moved in its orbit. The entrance locks to the great interior drydocks were gaping open and one of the locks was half blocked off with heaps of rubble.

Ben signaled Petro again. "I don't like this," he said. "Do you see any ships?"

"Not a one. But they may be inside."

"But there ought to be dozens here by now."

Petro grunted. "Let's move in closer," he said.

The Barrons were at the control panel now, staring at the image of destruction in the view screen. Cautiously Ben inched the little S-80 closer, searching the surface of the rock for signs of life. The SOS continued coming in, weakly but steadily.

"What are you waiting for?" Tom Barron asked. "Aren't you going to land?"

It was exactly the question Ben had been debating. It seemed the obvious thing to do, but a sharp edge of apprehension was holding him back. He looked up at Tom suddenly. "I don't know," he said. "Would you?"

"I'd certainly answer an SOS."

Ben grunted, studying the view screen again. It would be easy enough. A few deft maneuvers would bring the S-80 into alignment with the main entry lock. Then the standard grappling maneuvers would draw the little ship down with practically no impact onto the conveyor belt leading into the heart of the hollowed-out asteroid. A crew of Spacers ought to be on the alert to help grapple the ship and draw it in, closing down the pressure locks behind it. A simple matter, landing a ship on an outpost asteroid.

But Ben didn't start the maneuvers. Instead, he ran down the signal lights on the control panel, checking out his missile tubes and launching apparatus to see that they were operating.

"What's the matter?" Tom Barron asked.

"I don't like this," Ben said. "It's just too quiet down there."

"But it's obviously been attacked," Tom protested "There could be men dying down there."

"I know." For a moment Ben thought of the phantom ship that could not be seen, moving in with subtle menace to study his ship and course and then moving away again like a wraith.

"Why are you so eager?" he asked Tom Barron suddenly. "What makes you so sure there's anybody in there at all? Why the rush to go down there?"

Tom look chagrined. "I just thought you might be able to help, if—if somebody's been hurt."

Suspicion crystallized in Ben's mind. "Maybe," he said. "Or maybe you already know what's happened down there. Spies have been known to carry homing devices, hidden on their bodies. Maybe you've been in contact somehow with that ship we couldn't see."

"I never heard of that ship before," Tom cried angrily. "Use your head! Would I be calling in a ship that might blow us all to flinders? Including my sister and me?"

"Maybe you're just looking for a rescue," Ben countered. "Or maybe you figure it would be worth getting blown up just to put a Spacer ship out of commission. Maybe your own military would figure that was a worthwhile sacrifice, if they could wipe out a Spacer ship."

"You're crazy. Our pilots aren't bloodthirsty monsters." Tom looked at the view screen. "As far as I know, nobody at home even knew for sure that I was aboard your ship when you pulled away from the raid. And I haven't had any contact with anyone but you since."

Ben looked at the sandy-haired Earthman, and came to a decision. "Maybe not," he said. "But there's one way to be sure." He signaled Petro's ship. "I'm going down," he told the older Spacer. "Pull your ship back, well back, and cover me."

He waited while Petro's crippled ship drifted back away from him, then took the controls of the S-80 and nosed down toward the gaping hole of the outpost entry lock. The asteroid loomed larger in the view screen as Ben edged his ship closer; the SOS signal came through stronger by the moment.

And then, with his ship less than a thousand yards from the lock, the SOS stopped as abruptly as it had begun. A moment later Ben heard a cry from Petro as three cruiser-size Earth ships slid out from behind the asteroid, one on either side of him and one below.

He had walked straight into a ambush.

In the next few seconds Ben Trefon followed his reflexes with a swiftness he could never have copied by reason. He recognized the trap instantly; he was in a crossfire between the ships, with one avenue of escape cut off by the bulk of the asteroid. Landing, he knew, would be suicide. With a snarl he wrenched at the controls, twisting the little ship out of its smooth landing arc. Rockets flared from the belly of one of the Earth ships, and another turned a barrage of homing missiles out toward Petro's crippled cruiser.

"Run for it, Petro!" Ben shouted. "It's a trap!" In the same breath he turned to bring the nearest Earth ship into his hairline sights and fired three of his air-to-air missiles. Then without hesitation he fired his rear jets, nosing the S-80 down to follow the shells straight for the Earth ship's hull. Somewhere near the ship he saw two bright flares as his defensive missiles detonated the Earth ship's first barrage; moments later he was at close range with the hulking craft, firing off a swarm of wasps, the close-combat weapon that moved so swiftly and in such numbers that big defensive missiles could not stop them readily.

Two of the wasps struck the hull of the Earth ship, leaving a great gaping hole. Then two more struck, and then three more as Ben's ship jerked with the recoil. Suddenly something in the Earth ship exploded. Great billows of flame poured out of the ship as it began rolling end-over-end away from him.

"One down," Ben grated. "That leaves two to go."

He was swinging his ship around when another flare of light caught his eye, off in the distance where Petro's ship had been waiting. Frantically Ben signaled. There was no answer. Two more fireballs exploded from the crippled cruiser, major missile strikes, and the Spacer ship opened at the seams in dreadful slow motion. Fragments of hull flew out in all directions, only to be sucked back into the vortex of the fireball.

Numbly, Ben knew that Petro was gone, and the two remaining Earth ships were turning to converge their fire on him. "Strap down!" he shouted to the Barrons as he braced himself and seized the controls. Joyce went reeling back to the cots as Ben turned the ship in toward the flank of the closest Earth ship. But Tom Barron grabbed a shock bar and leaped into the weapon-control seat beside Ben.

"Get away from those guns," Ben snarled.

"Shut up and move this tub," Tom shot back at him. "Get it out of the crossfire. I'll handle these things."

Ben hesitated only an instant. Then he turned his full attention to the controls. The Earth ships were moving apart, trying to keep him in crossfire, and just as stubbornly he was moving out on the flank of the nearest one. If he could get one of the ships between him and the other, he would have only one ship to fight; homing missiles had no minds, and could not distinguish a friendly ship from a foe. The big Earth ship he was flanking seemed to recognize his intent. It started a lumbering turn, moving in toward its sister ship and holding its fire as it maneuvered. But the S-80 was lighter and faster. As the second ship emptied its missile tubes in a broadside barrage, Ben changed his plan. Swiftly, almost recklessly, he reversed direction, hurling himself and Tom up against the control panel as the null-grav units screamed in protest, and then dropped the S-80's nose sharply down between the two Earth ships.

Tom had been waiting for an opening. Now, with his hairline sights centered on the most distant Earth ship, he began triggering the forward shells. Ben edged the ship in toward the other, staying in a direct line between the two. A moment later a dozen wasps moved out from their tubes at the rear, wavered at the confusion of target signals, and turned sharply on the nearer Earth ship. A shell full of scrap metal burst from the Earth ship's tubes, scattering a wall of debris between them, and the S-80's wasps began detonating like firecrackers, out of contact range.

Tom reached for the switch to launch another barrage of wasps, but Ben stopped him.

"Hold onto those," he said. "Concentrate your fire on the farthest one."

"But you're getting too close to this one."

"I know what I'm doing. Get set to let the other one have a barrage."

The S-80 was close to the first Earth ship now, and closing in fast. But it was approaching on a side away from the missile tubes. Twice the great cruiser fired homing missiles, but the Spacer ship was too close, and the shells moved harmlessly out into space, finally homing on fragments of debris. Tom Barron was staring at the view screen now as the cruiser loomed up alarmingly. "Ben! You're going to ram him!"

"Not quite." Poised for the right instant, Ben slammed down the null-grav switches when the ship was just a few feet from the cruiser. Grappling plates shot out on cables from the S-80's hull and clanged down on the hull of the Earth ship. "Get that other one, *now!* He can't fire on us without blowing his pal here to pieces."

Tom worked the weapon controls in a kind of frenzy, firing wasps one at a time to break through the cruiser's defenses. The Earth ship saw its predicament: it couldn't fire back, and soon the wasps would exhaust its defensive missiles. For a moment the cruiser lay immobile and vulnerable; then as Tom fired three waves of heavy warhead missiles it seemed to gather its wits and tried to scurry clumsily out of the way of the oncoming shells. But it was too late. With defensive shells exhausted, two of the S-80's missiles took the ship broadside. There was a mighty orange flare in the center of the ship; it seemed to split down the middle, the fragments breaking into still smaller fragments as the cruiser disintegrated.

"Good boy," Ben said. "That evens the odds a little. Now let's see what we can do with our friends here."

He released the grappling plates. With a burst of side jets the Spacer craft jumped away from the cruiser's hull. The Earth ship was waiting; with the S-80 so close she was helpless to attack, but the instant the Spacer ship cast off the cruiser moved around with amazing agility.

"They're centering on us," Tom cried out. "You'd better move this thing."

"Hold on." Ben hit the forward power, trying to slip in behind the asteroid for cover. But the Earth ship was already moving to block the maneuver. Missiles broke free from half a dozen forward tubes and sped toward the Spacer craft, keeping Tom busy launching counter missiles. Once again Ben tried to move so that the asteroid lay between him and the enemy, but the Earth ship was too nimble.

Ben glanced at Tom nervously. "How are our shells holding up?"

"They're going fast. We'll be in trouble pretty soon," Tom said, checking the storage dials.

"Then use the wasps as much as you can. And the forward tubes have a couple of loads of scrap."

As he talked, Ben was watching the movement of the Earth ship. This craft was not maneuvering clumsily like the other two. The pilot seemed to know his ship's capabilities. More important, his thinking was uncomfortably in line with Ben's, for he was anticipating every move Ben made. The two ships were circling the outpost asteroid now, with Ben trying desperately to get the great rock between him and the cruiser, while the Earth ship was equally determined not to let the Spacer craft out of its sights.

Ben worked the controls frantically as move was matched by counter-move. At every opportunity the cruiser was firing; sooner or later, Ben knew, a shell would get past the wasps, or the S-80's supply of defensive weapons would be exhausted. He ducked the ship down close to the asteroid surface, watched as a warhead from the cruiser was caught by the magnetic bulk of the rock, deflected out of its homing course to detonate harmlessly on the surface.

It gave Ben an idea. For all of its pilot's skill, the Earth ship was bigger, its reaction time slower than the little S-80. Ben fired his forward jets, moving his ship out in a great arc away from the asteroid. As he anticipated, the Earth ship moved out on his tail, following him doggedly as if waiting for the kill that was certain to come. Away from the rock, the Earth ship accelerated, moving in swiftly. Then, with side jets roaring, Ben cut his arc short and dropped the S-80's nose back down to skim the surface of the asteroid.

This move took the cruiser by surprise. The Earth ship had been following him move for move; once again it followed suit. Intent on its prey, the pilot had momentarily forgotten the asteroid itself and cut his ship's arc too short as he curved in to follow the Spacer. The cruiser's pilot saw his error too late. Without the deft maneuverability of the Spacer craft, the Earth ship crashed broadside into the jagged rock surface of the asteroid, turned a great end-over-end flip and crashed down again, crumbling its main power jets. Ponderously the ship began to ricochet; grappling plates shot out toward the surface of the rock and the wounded vessel crunched down once again, raising a shower of dust and rock fragments in a halo around it.

Ben crowed in triumph, moving his little ship back for a better view. As he balanced the ship's power at a distance of eight hundred yards, the Barrons crowded around him at the view screen.

"Got his tubes," Ben said. "That's why he grappled. He knew he'd be a helpless cripple off the surface."

"You don't think he can move?" Joyce asked.

"I think he would if he could. He knows we've still got fire power. If he could be running for it, he would be." Ben stared in silence at the wreck below. "That was quite a trap," he said finally. "They must have knocked out the outpost early in the game, and then just sucked in every Spacer ship that came along."

"Well, it was a trap that didn't work," Tom said shakily. "He's not going to chase you, and the other two ships are done for. You might as well get out of here before he calls for help."

Ben scratched his jaw and continued to stare at the view screen. "Somebody must have survived the crash in order to throw out the grapplers."

"Okay, why not let them alone?" Tom said. "They're not going to hurt another Spacer ship. You could smash them to pieces with one shell, but what's the use? That ship isn't going to ambush anybody again."

Ben shook his head. "I wasn't thinking of firing on them," he said. "I just don't like leaving them. Seems to me you Earthmen once had a law of the woods, back when you had forests full of game. The law said that when you wound an animal, you go in after him." He sat down at the controls, and began easing the ship down toward the wreckage of the Earth ship.

Tom and Joyce exchanged glances. "You've got room enough for a few survivors on this ship," Joyce said. "They won't give you any trouble."

"I hope not." Ben altered his course a little, peering at the view screen. He beamed a recognition signal, but there was no answer from the wrecked ship. He dropped lower, to within two hundred yards, and then began settling the S-80 gently down toward the battered hull.

He was within fifty yards of the surface when Tom let out a cry, and Ben saw the blunt muzzles of two missile tubes near the front of the wounded ship swivel upward. Ben's hand shot out to the braking controls, reversing direction as the missile tubes coughed flame and two shells snaked up toward the Spacer ship like deadly arrows. The reverse slammed them against the control panel; frantically Ben triggered defensive shells from the rear tubes, but he knew as he did so that it was too late. Even if they stopped the cruiser's shells before contact, they would take the full force of the concussion wave.

"Down!" he shouted. "Fast!" Leaping to his feet he caught Joyce Barron by the shoulders and hurled her to the deck beneath the acceleration cots. Tom dove for the deck on the other side of the cabin, arms covering his head. Ben hesitated just long enough to throw off the ship's main power switch and then himself turned to hit the deck.

But his last move had taken a split second too long. Even as he turned he heard the deafening crash of the detonation. The rear bulkhead of the cabin bulged inward like a metal bubble and burst along its seams; something struck him a blow on the head as he fell forward to the deck. In that last second he saw an orange inferno behind the split bulkhead, felt himself picked up and hurled backward by the concussion wave and dumped in a heap against the control panel. There was pain and searing heat and blinding light as he lost consciousness.

But the greatest pain of all in that instant was the bitter realization that he had allowed himself to be trapped again.

7 DERELICT

SOMEWHERE far in the distance a hammer was pounding on steel, a steady, nerve-shattering din that seemed to have been going on for hours. Slowly, fighting every inch of the way, Ben Trefon dragged himself up into consciousness, wishing desperately that the pounding would cease. Presently he blinked his eyes open, staring around him at the sheet-draped cubicle and fighting down an almost overwhelming wave of helplessness and confusion. It was then that he realized that the pounding was not in the distance at all. It was going on right inside his own head.

Shakily he gripped the edge of the cot and tried to sit up. The pounding in his head picked up speed, and a searing pain shot through his chest and right shoulder. Now he became aware of bulky gauze bandages half covering him. He sank back with a groan, trying to orient himself.

Vaguely he remembered being awake a few times before, for a few moments. Little fragments of clouded memory flooded his mind. Once he had awakened in darkness to hear the muffled throbbing of engines somewhere below him, a throbbing edged with a high-pitched, uneasy whine. Another time there had been light and movement, with the sound of hushed voices, and the feeling of cool moist packs bathing his forehead. Again, a memory of the sharp bite of a needle in his arm, the glitter of an intravenous bottle on a stand above his head, and a soft feminine voice that had sounded incredibly sweet in its reassurance. And through it all, like a red haze, there was the continuing impression of pain and aching in his shoulder and chest and the inability—or unwillingness—to move.

Now alarm flared in his mind. How long had he been unconscious? Where was he, and what was happening? There was a vivid memory of the crippled Earth ship firing upon him as he tried to move to its assistance, waiting until he was in point-blank range. There was the fearful realization that the little S-80 was hit, and the bitter knowledge that he had been trapped once again by a cruel and ruthless enemy, or by an enemy so blinded by fear that it fought back with any vicious weapon at its disposal. And now the sheets draping his cot were hanging from familiar overhead wires, and the wall beside his cot was certainly the wall of the S-80's bunk room.

Suddenly light flooded the cubicle and Joyce Barron was looking in at him, her sandy hair tousled, a tray in one hand. "Well," she said. "So you finally decided to wake up and take nourishment."

Once again Ben tried to sit up. "Take it easy," the girl said. "Tom will be here in a minute to help you."

"But we've got to get away from them."

"Don't worry, we're safe now. But you'll go flat on your face if you try to walk. You did that once already. And try not to move your shoulder. I don't think anything's broken, but there's still a lot of drainage."

"Drainage!" Ben looked down at the bulky dressing. "What happened to me? Shrapnel? How long have I been out like this?"

"About four days."

"Four *days!!*"

"Well, we're not sure. The silly chronometer hasn't been working right all the time. But that's pretty close."

By gripping the shock bar at the edge of the cot, Ben managed to stagger to his feet. He paused for a wave of dizziness to pass, then tottered out into the cabin against Joyce's protests, feeling like an old, old man.

He could hardly believe what he saw.

The ship was under power, no doubt about it. The radar scanner was making its monotonous sweep, emitting a cheerful *beep* at the end of each circuit. The rear bulkhead, torn open from top to bottom, was sealed tight with a sheet of plastic. While he was still staring the rear hatchway banged open and Tom Barron came through from the storeroom, his arms stacked high with provisions and boxes of electrical equipment.

"Well," the Earthman said, dumping his load on the floor. "So the Sleeping Beauty finally woke up. It took that kiss a long time to work."

"Never mind the humor," Joyce said. "Just get him sitting down before he passes out again. Then maybe he can show you how those silly circuits are supposed to work."

Leaning on Tom's arm, Ben staggered across the cabin and into the seat behind the control panel. The ship was operational, beyond question, even though he knew the blast had come directly through the engine rooms. Tom checked something on a sheaf of papers, and adjusted the controls with the air of a bride making her first cake. The ship jerked roughly as it shifted course.

"You've got it running!" Ben said in amazement.

"Oh, it's *running,* all right," Tom said. "But that's about all. I couldn't make head nor tail of those null-gravity circuits, and we spent about three hours turning end-over-end until I got us stabilized with the side jets, but we're on a steady course now even if we can't develop any power."

"What kind of a course?"

"I'm not sure," Tom said dubiously. "Roughly away from the sun, and more or less in the direction of your Asteroid Central. At least I *think* that's where we're headed." He waved a hand wearily at the ship's computer. "Your gadget there and I have been going round and round. But once I figured out how to tape information into the miserable thing, I began to get somewhere plotting a course. Trouble is, we keep veering off it all the time. Either I can't add or the computer can't."

Ben peered at Tom's pages of calculations, and began to check the ship's dials. Tom's technique was awkward, but his answers were amazingly accurate. Ben looked up at him. "How long did we wander under power before you got your figures straight?"

"Quite some time, maybe seventeen or eighteen hours," Tom said. "I was pretty slow."

"Well, that might account for the drift. The computer assumes the ship is in the plane of the ecliptic unless you tape in correction data. We must have drifted about eighty degrees off the ecliptic while you were calculating. But that shouldn't cause a lot of deviation from course."

"Then something else is causing it," Tom said. "I have to correct every ten minutes. It seems as if something is pushing us off course steadily in the same direction."

"Well, whatever it is, we'll fix it. You've done all right for a city slicker." It was an understatement, and Ben knew it. What Tom had done was little short of miraculous for one without training or experience. "But what happened to the Earth ship?"

Tom Barron's mouth set in a hard line. "We had a couple of shells left. I used them. If I hadn't been so mad I would have used wasps instead, but I just emptied the tubes at them. So don't worry, they won't shoot down anybody else that tries to help them."

"But your own people!"

"I'm sorry, but I can't claim them. They knew you were trying to help them. If you'd planned to hurt them you'd never have started to land. They deliberately waited until you couldn't veer off, and then let you have it." The Earthman shook his head. "Okay, they made their choice, and I made mine. As it was, they almost succeeded. The shrapnel tore through a corner of the engine room and split open this rear bulkhead. You got hit in the neck and shoulder, and you took a piece in the chest as well. I'm no doctor, but I got two big pieces out of your shoulder, and sealed off the hole in your chest, and spent a few hours picking cinders out of your scalp. Then Joyce took over the nursing care—she was in training back home before this started. And if you try to tell me we did wrong, I'll gladly blow some shrapnel back into you myself."

"Okay, okay," Ben said. "Relax. You'd better show me the damage to the ship."

Inch by inch he went over the ship with Tom. "I've been working on it as fast as I could," Tom said. "I got the holes in the hull patched up, or welded, or both. The jet engines were damaged, but the main jets worked pretty well once I got a crack in the combustion chamber welded shut. The only trouble is that the engine temp starts going up every time I try to throw on any power."

Ben shuddered. Jet combustion chambers were built to critical tolerances; sometimes in testing them the tiniest flaw could blow an engine to fragments. "I'm glad I was unconscious during all this," he said. "You must have a guardian angel."

They went on with the inspection. The more Ben saw, the more difficult it was to believe. It was a miracle that they were alive in the first place, and as much of a miracle that there was anything left at all of the ship's engine room. But most miraculous of all, it seemed to Ben, was the thing that Tom Barron had left unspoken. With Ben wounded and unconscious on the cabin floor, there was nothing to prevent Tom Barron and his sister from moving the ship out of range of the wounded Earth ship's missiles and then establishing radio contact with them, identifying themselves as Earthmen and demanding to be taken aboard. Ben struggled with the thought, still searching for hidden motives, but he could find none.

There was only one possible answer. The Barrons had made their decision. Even if they did not say so in so many words, they had unmistakably thrown in their lot with Ben and the Spacers.

And that meant that now they too were outlaws, and for the same reason that the earliest Spacers had become outlaws: because they had been unwilling to take part in an idiotic war, a war that they saw to be pointless and foolish. Somehow the Barrons had realized that the source of their fears had been superstition and ignorance. And once they had realized that the Spacers lived the way they did just to survive, that there were no monster regiments and mutated horrors ready to invade their home planet, they had begun to recognize this war between Earthmen and Spacers for what it really was—a pointless and hysterical reaction to the shadowy fears that had been festering in the minds of Earthmen for centuries.

Back in the control room, Ben and Tom held a council of war. "You've done splendidly," Ben said, "but we're literally sitting on a powder keg. Those engines won't hold up without a thorough overhaul. We can fix them so we can limp along to drydock somewhere, but we don't even dare limp very far without some work on them. We've just got to kill our power and improvise something before the engines go out altogether."

Tom hesitated. "Isn't there some place we can take cover while we're doing that? Some place we can't be spotted so easily as just sitting out here in the middle of nothing without any power?"

Something in his voice made Ben look up. "Are you worrying about Earth ships spotting us?"

"Well, there's that. . . ."

"But there's something else, too, isn't there?"

Tom nodded. "I might have been mistaken, but there was a time a few hours ago when I was sure we'd picked up our invisible friends again."

"You mean the phantom ship?"

"At least, something I couldn't pick up on the 'scope. The radar picked it up for just a minute or two, and then lost it again. Of course, the explosion might have jarred some wires loose in the radar and given me a false signal for a while. But it was just about that time that the ship began this business of drifting off course."

Ben looked skeptical. "That's hard to swallow," he said. "There isn't any known way for a ship at a distance to alter the course of another ship without having a remote control governor on the responding ship's engines. And I *know* there isn't any governor aboard this ship . . . I'd have seen it while we were inspecting just now."

"There couldn't be some kind of unit you overlooked?" Tom asked.

"I've been working with rocket engines since I was five," Ben said. "I'd have noticed anything that didn't belong there in a minute." He laughed at Tom's sober expression. "So you're just chasing a red herring. The drive engines are merely out of alignment."

"Maybe," Tom said, obviously still unconvinced. He stared angrily at the tracer map, still showing a steady deviation of the ship from the charted course. With Ben watching he again adjusted back to the course. Within minutes the little ship had again veered off. "But I still wonder just where this ship would go if we quit adjusting back to *our* course."

"Probably nowhere," Ben said. "Eventually, of course, we'd come within contact range of some asteroid or other, but there isn't a chance in a million that we'd actually be *heading* for one right now."

Tom sat silent for a moment. Then he said, "Just on a long shot, why don't you check and see?"

"Sure, if you're really worried." Ben began taking co-ordinate readings from the control panel at one minute intervals for about ten minutes and taped them into the computer. The ship's deviation from course wasn't great, but it was consistent. Next Ben hauled out a tape marked "Co-ordinates of the Asteroids" for the current year. A few moments later he had taped the deviating course of the ship into the computer for comparison with the orbits of known asteroids in their present segment of space.

The computer clicked busily for a few moments, and dropped a card down into the slot. Ben picked it up, and stared. Then he handed it over to Tom, frowning. "Okay, there you are. If we stop correcting and let the ship follow the course it's taking, we'll be in contact course with a major-sized asteroid in about three hours."

Tom whistled. "Then something *is* pushing us off course!"

"Either that, or it's a million-to-one coincidence," Ben said gloomily. "Of course, there are lots of asteroids, and it could be just happenstance."

"But you doubt it," Tom said.

"In space you don't believe in coincidences. In any event, we'll soon know. We need a landfall to allow us to repair the engines. If somebody wants us to land in a certain place, maybe we'd better let ourselves be shoved around for a while. Because if there's a ship out there that's trying to make us go somewhere, the sooner we call its bluff the better."

The calculation of travel time to the asteroid was surprisingly accurate. In just a few minutes less than three hours the S-80's radar picked up the huge rock fragment in its scanning sweep, one of the ragged chunks of cosmic debris that were to be found scattered far and wide throughout the Asteroid Belt. Their target had no name, and according to the most recent almanacs in the ship's tape library, it had never been landed upon nor explored. It had merely been observed from a distant scout ship at some time in the past, its orbit calculated and its position relative to Asteroid Central at that moment in time recorded. Thereafter, its position had been checked by the astronomers on Asteroid Central once every twenty years, and the minute orbital changes entered on the record of asteroid co-ordinates.

As asteroids went, it was neither large nor small, utterly undistinguished as it made its silent, endless passage around the sun. But now Ben Trefon scanned its surface closely, automatically checking in his mind the physical qualities necessary for a useful landfall: the general size and shape of the rock, its stability on its axis, the nature of its surface. As the asteroid slowly rotated before them on the view screen, the entire surface was exposed to the sun's light. It was forty miles in diameter, almost spherical except for one flattened side, and covered with small surface rubble.

Finally Ben nodded. "It'll do, as far as a landfall is concerned. As for a reception committee—if they're there, they're staying well hidden." He scanned the surface through another complete rotation. Then he nosed the little S-80 downward. "It looks deserted. But keep your hands on the wasp controls just the same."

Tom manned the weapons controls as Ben pulled his blouse tighter around his chest and tried to adjust his sore shoulder to ease the steady aching. Suddenly he was aware of the black belt around his waist. It seemed tighter than before, and for a moment he thought he felt an almost imperceptible vibration from the capsule lodged within it. Then he shrugged in disgust. It was only his own muscle tension as he gripped the controls. "Hold on," he said. "We're going down."

Slowly the little ship drifted down toward the surface of the rock. All three of them were tense now, hardly breathing as

Ben brought the ship in for a smooth and graceful landing at precisely the same orbital velocity as the asteroid. There was hardly a jar as they touched down; Ben sent out the grappling plates, watched them as they slithered along the surface to lodge tightly into crevices in the iron-bearing rock. Ben touched the ship's power momentarily to strain at the cables, making certain that the ship was firmly secured to the surface with no possibility of settling or shift. Then he killed power and sat back, a fine line of perspiration on his forehead.

Nothing happened. The view screen showed a ragged, barren surface, the horizon unexpectedly close. Beyond the rim of rock a million stars blazed, tiny pinpoints of light, and the sun inched slowly down in the black sky to be hidden behind the rock as it rotated on its axis.

But there was no sign of life, no ship suddenly appearing in the sky. . . .

No reception committee.

For a full hour they waited, hardly moving from their seats, as though expecting a time bomb to go off. And then, suddenly, the tension broke and the three of them were roaring with laughter, practically hugging each other in relief. "Talk about a bunch of frightened old ladies!" Tom Barron said. "Joyce, I'm starved. Get us something to eat while I break out the pressure suits. The sun ought to be around again in another half hour. And if something jumps out of the shadows at you, be sure to scream."

They ate hungrily. Ben's appetite had been voracious ever since he had regained consciousness, and even the dull fare of shipboard rations seemed exceedingly tasty. But both he and Tom were eager to get to work. During transit they had made a list of the major repairs necessary in order of their importance; now they spent an hour or so hauling tools from the repair locker, sharpening drills, checking the tolerances of the machining tools and getting ready for the first job.

The engines, of course, took precedence. Opened seams had to be power-clamped, braised and welded, and then reground. The null-grav units had cracked open just enough to leak gyroscope lubricant all over the engine room. It took several hours of greasy work to get each unit resealed, and then tested out under full power. Tom handled the cable controls to hold the units down as each of the six gyros was tested individually; another hour of work was required to get all six into perfect timing so that the null-gravity was imperceptible to the human occupants in the ship, and so that resonance between the units did not develop with its steel-shattering vibration.

Tom and Ben worked, ate and slept in regular rotation, trying to plan work periods to take advantage of the asteroid's brightside hours. Joyce undertook some wiring repair, but for the most part she just got meals and grew bored. After a few hours of clanging hammers, roaring drills and the brassy rattle of riveting guns going on all sides of her, she told the boys she was going to explore a bit between meals.

At Ben's insistence the first reconnaissance was made by the three of them together, so that he could check the integrity of their pressure suits and see that Joyce got the hang of travel with magnetic boots on a virtually gravity-less surface. For Tom and Joyce it was a strange experience indeed to feel their boots grab the ragged terrain, to talk by pressing their helmets together when they got tired of using radio communication, and to walk the surface of a planetoid with the horizon just a stone's throw away. The asteroid was a place of darkness and shadow even in full sunlight; its solitude and silence were unnerving at first. Ben watched his Earthling friends out of the corner of his eye for any evidence of the panic reaction that the most hardened Spacers sometimes experienced on asteroid landings, but the Barrons seemed to adjust to the strange landfall without difficulty.

After that Joyce was free to explore while Ben and Tom worked. But she found other things to do as well. She found the tape library an endless source of pleasure, with the microfilmed books from the Spacer archives on Asteroid Central, and the hundreds of music tapes Ben had stored over the years. More than once he found her listening entranced to the recorded songs of the maukis . . . the chants and laments, the battle songs and lullabies that Ben had known since birth. Nothing seemed to relieve the loneliness and tension so quickly as music, but to the Barrons the mauki songs were subtly different from the songs and symphonies they had known at home on Earth.

"It's such *mournful* singing," Joyce said on one occasion when Ben found her listening. "Even the marches and victory songs give you a funny feeling."

"Funny in what way?"

"Funny-peculiar. As if something were missing. I can't put my finger on the right word."

"Maybe you mean homesickness," Ben said. "You don't find it on the surface, but it's there, buried in every song.

Even in the victory songs. I guess the one thing all Spacers have always wanted to do was to go home."

Joyce nodded. "Maybe that's it," she said. "After all, there hasn't ever really been a Spacer victory, has there? But the singing is beautiful. Even in the laments there's no hint of begging or self-pity." She looked up at Ben. "Your people must be very proud."

"Anyone who lives in space is proud," Ben Trefon said. "We have a right to be. But we also have hope of someday going home again. That's what the maukis are singing about, really. An exile can be proud and still hope to see the end of his exile."

"But with the horrible things Earthmen believe about Spacers, it's hard to see the end, even if this war were over," Joyce said. "If there were only some way to tell people the truth . . . all of them, all at once."

"Well, there isn't any way, and that's that. The truth has to be believed, to do any good. And the war isn't over, and if our encounter at Outpost 5 is any guide, it won't be over for a while. And we won't be any help unless we get this tub back together again." Ben paused. "Find anything interesting on your jaunts outside?"

"Not much, but I'll keep poking around. It's a fascinating place to explore, especially since we know goblins aren't going to get us."

Ben chuckled and went back to his work. Bit by bit the three of them had been forgetting their caution. Since landfall there had been no sign of anything wrong about this planetoid . . . no ambush, no hidden ships, nothing. Ben's initial uneasiness at having Joyce exploring the surface alone had given way to a certain satisfaction that she took to the discomforts of pressure suit confinement so well and seemed to enjoy her explorations. At least, he reflected, it gave her something to do while the tedious repair work went on. After each jaunt she had a new account of the nooks and crannies of the ragged surface she had investigated. Now even her brother was remarking half jokingly that she was taking to space like a born Spacer.

For Ben and Tom the work was exhausting and absorbing, as the damage to the ship was repaired bit by bit. With Joyce happy at other things, they both occasionally forgot meals. But the day that the final tests and timing adjustments on the main jets were done both boys worked halfway around the clock before they realized that Joyce had not been back for several hours.

"Probably down in one of her fool gullies," Tom said sourly. "One of these times she's going to get a foot caught and we'll have to go haul her out."

Ben nodded. "I suppose we'll have to lay down the law," he said. "We only have a couple of more days of work here. It'd be a pity to have her losing her bearings and getting lost, or breaking a leg or something." He glanced at the chronometer. "Anyway, I'm hungry. Let's find something to eat."

They fixed a meal and finished it in silence. Still Joyce didn't appear. "Maybe we should signal her," Tom said. "She wouldn't have gone out of straight beam range."

Ben tapped out a signal that Joyce should pick up, but there was no response. They waited a while longer, growing more uneasy by the minute. Finally Ben said, "Well, I suppose we'd better go out and see what's happened."

"You don't suppose she's gotten hurt?"

"I don't know how. But she must be gone for six hours now." Together, they climbed into pressure suits, and dropped down to the ragged surface below the entry hatch. The sun was directly overhead now, so that the surface was visible from horizon to horizon. There was no sign of Joyce. But off to the right there was a promontory of rock affording a better view.

They had just started across toward the rock when the glint of a pressure suit helmet appeared over a rock ledge to the left of them, and Joyce came into view, scrambling through the rubble. But she was not returning at a normal, casual pace. She was running, or trying to run, fighting to disengage her magnetic boots and tripping over them in her haste. For a moment she stopped to look back over her shoulder, and then came stumbling and falling down the path toward them, catching herself on rocks and picking herself up again to hurry on. Ben's earphones picked up the sound of gasping breathing mixed with frightened sobs; then she saw them, and was screaming for Tom in a voice filled with terror.

Tom gave Ben a swift glance and rushed across the rocks to meet his sister. She fell into his arms, her words coming so fast that Ben couldn't catch them as he moved slowly toward the pair. When Joyce saw him she clutched her brother even closer, her eyes wide with horror. "Don't let him come near," she sobbed. "Keep him away, Tom, don't let him come near. This time we're the ones that are trapped, just because we listened to this—this traitor!"

Ben stared at Tom, his jaw sagging. Tom shook his sister.

"What are you talking about?" he said. "Get hold of yourself! What do you mean?"

"I mean I *saw* them, that's what I mean!" The girl's voice rose hysterically. "He's been lying to us all the time! They're here, I saw them, back there in the rocks. They were standing there staring at me . . . and he said there weren't any such things!"

"Any such *whats?*"

"Monsters," Joyce Barron gasped. "Horrible mutant monsters." She turned to glare at Ben Trefon. "You can stop lying to us now, because it won't do any good any more. You people have an army of monsters, all right. I've seen them with my own eyes. And this horrible rock is alive with them!"

8 THE CLEFT IN THE ROCK

FOR THE FIRST moment Ben Trefon could hardly credit his ears. He stood staring at the girl as her words tumbled out. She couldn't really mean what she was saying, he thought, but there was no mistaking the words. Even though she was not making sense, he had heard her with perfect clarity. And from the scornful look on her face, she was not joking in the least.

Ben shook his head in confusion. "Wait a minute," he said. "'Just slow down and wait a minute. What are you talking about?"

Joyce clung to her brother's arm. "I'm talking about monsters," she said. "I saw them back there—three, four, maybe a dozen. Horrible little things three feet high with gray skin and wrinkles and eyes like fire." Her voice was unsteady as she tried to keep from sobbing.

"Take it easy, now," Tom said gently. "Pull yourself together. You mean that you actually saw something?"

"Of course I saw something!" Joyce Barron wailed. "What do you think I'm saying? They're all around back there. For all I know we could be surrounded right now."

For a moment the thought of space fever crossed Ben's mind. Every Spacer knew that this kind of irrational breakdown could occur as a result of isolation for long periods in the loneliness of space. Sometimes the pressures of just staying alive in the face of a hostile environment could become overwhelming and break forth in hallucinations and hysteria. Ben had spent two weeks on a ship with a man who had broken down in such a fashion during his training school days, but there had been clues to what was coming for days before the break occurred. It was impossible to believe that such a thing could strike out of the blue without the slightest warning, unless Joyce Barron were a far better actress than Ben thought she was.

There was only one alternative: that Joyce actually *had* seen something that nearly frightened her out of her wits. A rock formation, some movement of shadows on the asteroid surface, perhaps a shifting of the surface rubble under the influence of the asteroid's barely measurable gravity—whatever it was, there was only one way to deal with it. "If you really think you saw something," Ben said, "then tell us what. Not what you *think* you saw, I mean what you *really* saw."

"As if you don't know perfectly well," the girl said bitterly. "And to think we believed all your talk about the poor, mistreated Spacers and their good intentions!"

"All right, let's get that straight first," Ben said. "Maybe you did see something, but if you did it was nothing I know anything about. There aren't any Spacer mutants. We don't have any monsters bottled up in caves anywhere." He looked at Tom. "Maybe I can't make you believe that, but it just happens to be true all the same."

"Then what did she see?" Tom said.

"I don't have the vaguest idea," Ben replied. "But believe me, if it was three feet tall with gray skin and wrinkles I want to see it too. I've been on a hundred of these rocks, and I've never seen anything alive on one yet. If there *is* something living here, we'd better find out about it fast."

Something in his voice must have told, for a little of the terror and bitterness in the girl's face softened. "There was something there, all right," she said. "I was following the trail I made around that spur of rock over there, looking for some more of the crystals I found over there yesterday. I was working to shake loose a piece that was wedged into the rock when something made me look up and I saw this face staring down at me. It just sat there and looked at me, and then all of a sudden it was gone."

"Couldn't it have been a rock formation?" Ben asked. "Sometimes these rocks move without anybody touching them."

"Have you ever seen a rock with blue eyes?" Joyce said. "That *blinked?* It was no rock, it was an ugly, horrible thing with long spindly arms and little crooked legs. And then as soon as I moved I saw two or three more scurrying back into the rocks."

Ben looked up at Tom and shook his head. "I think we'd just better have a look," he said.

"Well, you're not going to get me back there," Joyce said firmly.

"I'm afraid we are. You've got to show us where you saw these—these creatures, and which way they went." Ben found a locker key in his pocket, tossed it to Tom. "Go open my foot locker," he said. "You'll find your revolver there, and a couple of tangle-guns."

Tom disappeared into the ship and emerged a moment later with the weapons. He caught Ben's eye and drew him aside. "Do you really think we're going to find anything?"

Ben shook his head. "I don't see how. There's no atmosphere on these rocks, and nothing even remotely resembling food. I hate to say it, but I think your sister's imagination got out of control. Somehow she fooled herself into thinking she saw something that she didn't see at all."

But he didn't quite feel the conviction of his words. There was another thought in his mind which Ben just couldn't shake off. Of course there was non-human life in many parts of the solar system. Mars had an abundance of desert life: little gopher-like creatures that lived in burrows in the sand, tiny sand-snails that could dissolve sandstone for the algae living in its crevices, even the Jumping Jacks that could bound twenty feet in the air and travel at enormous speed across the dunes like a cross between the kangaroo and the jack rabbit. He had seen the Venusian mud-puppies that thrived in the steaming bogs of the second planet, and the strange pterodactyl-like birds with leathery wings that skimmed through the thin methane atmosphere of Saturn's Titan, settling down like Satanic demons in rows on the rocks to watch Spacer exploring parties.

An abundance of life, but never before had any life of any kind been found on the asteroids, particularly three-foot creatures with gray skins and horrible eyes. Ben could not even think of any living creature he had ever encountered that might fit that description. What Joyce had said she had seen was impossible, unless there was some form of life here that had never been detected.

Or that had just recently come. . . .

Again Ben's mind snagged on the thought he had been trying to avoid, a thought that nagged at him now as the three of them started down the trail Joyce pointed out. An invisible phantom ship, Ben thought, that made contact, and watched us, and then slipped away out of reach as soon as it was seen. A ship that returned again, perhaps, while he was unconscious following the explosion, and then began mysteriously nudging them into a course that led to this rock. He shook his head impatiently. It was a disturbing thought, but it made no sense, no sense at all.

No more sense than Joyce's little gray men.

Tom led the way, with Joyce at his heels, and Ben bringing

up the rear. They reached the great promontory of rock just as the sun slid into view from behind the rock, throwing long black shadows across the valley below them. Here the surface was strewn with giant boulders; Tom picked his way with care as Joyce pointed the way, and Ben's grip tightened on the tangle-gun at ready in his hand. As they started down Ben felt his tension increase a hundredfold; it seemed as if his whole body were vibrating, and his skin prickled as he peered down at the valley floor for signs of life.

Soon they were clambering down into a ravine, and Joyce stopped, staring up at a rock with a crack running down its surface. In the crack a large quartz crystal was tightly wedged. "This is the place," the girl said. "And over there is where I saw the first one."

They followed her finger, peering around them as if they expected the rocks themselves to leap into the air. There was no movement, no suggestion of life. Joyce scrambled around the rock. "Yes, this is the place! That crevice over there was where the others disappeared, or was it this one?" She stopped in confusion. "Well, it was somewhere over there," she said angrily. "I was too scared to see straight. It doesn't matter, anyway. They were here, that's all that matters."

The sun had swung high in the sky and was descending rapidly again toward the far horizon. Tom Barron gave an embarrassed cough. "Look, Ben, I think we'd better get back to the ship before it's dark again, don't you?"

"But I tell you *I saw them!*" Joyce burst out. "You both think I'm crazy, but I'm not."

"I think we've looked far enough," Tom said.

But Ben Trefon shook his head. "Let's see where that crevice goes before we go back," he said. Something was still bothering him; the closer he had come to this place, the greater his tension had been growing. Now it seemed as though his body were trembling uncontrollably. His feet were actually unsteady as he started to scramble across the floor of the ravine toward the cleft in the rock, and his heart seemed to be pounding a thousand times a minute.

And then, quite suddenly, he realized that it was not his heart pounding, and not his body that was vibrating. He stopped suddenly and pressed his glove over the capsule in his belt.

There was no doubt about it. The capsule was emitting a vibration so powerful it was shaking his body with an insistent pulsating beat. The beat was so intense that the capsule almost felt alive at his side.

Tom Barron stopped behind him. "Ben, we'd better go back."

"Not yet." Ben was scrambling forward now, staring at the cleft that loomed up ahead. Step by step the vibration in the capsule intensified as he stumbled in the rocky path.

Then, without warning, a tiny gray creature was standing in his path. Ben stopped short. Joyce had not been imagining things; the creature was barely three feet tall, with a wrinkled silvery-gray skin that made it look like a little old man. Its head was tilted to one side as if it were listening intently, and it stood perfectly motionless as Ben stared.

Tom caught up with him, and Ben heard a swift intake of breath. A stone rattled under Ben's foot. Abruptly the creature turned sharply toward him, and Ben saw his eyes, luminous eyes of a pale iridescent blue.

For a moment Ben thought the creature was blind, for the eyes had no pupils nor whites. Then he saw little flecks of gold shimmering in the pale blue, and he knew that the creature could see him. But the horror and ugliness Joyce had described had been the product of her own mind, for this tiny creature was far from ugly. Rather, there was an other-worldly beauty about him as he solemnly regarded his discoverers. He reminded Ben of something, something he had read of, or heard of, years before. But it was Tom who found the right word.

"Why, he looks like an elf!" he breathed.

Ben nodded. "Joyce was right, but there's nothing horrible about him." The same instant the creature moved closer. To Ben's amazement, *it spoke to him.* There were no audible words, no sound at all, yet somehow Ben heard a soft, musical voice speaking directly into his ear.

"The belt," the voice said. "Who has it?"

"I do," Ben blurted out.

The creature fixed its great eyes on him. "Then step forward, please."

Cautiously, Ben took a step ahead. The creature moved close, extended a hand to Ben's waist. Ben felt the gentlest touch, and the creature stepped back again. "Yes, you wear the belt of power. We have been waiting for you, and your companions as well. You are called Benjamin in the mighty House of Trefon, is that not so?"

Ben nodded. "But how did you know?"

"We knew your father well," the strange voice said. "We knew him long ago when he wore the belt. And now that it is in your hands, the time has come for you to use it, if it is not too late. We have waited a long time for you."

"But why? Who are you?"

"Who can say?" the voice replied softly in Ben's ear, and somehow the creature seemed to be smiling. "I am one who has been, and gone, and come again. You saw my ship once, when it was not intended. But come, we must not talk here. Your friends also may come, if they come in peace."

The creature turned as if to go, but Ben didn't move. "I want to know who you are," he said. "And I want to know what you want with us, before we go anywhere."

The tiny creature looked at him. "We want peace," the voice said in Ben's ear. "Would your father have given you the belt of power if he had not wanted us to find you? We have followed you across space for days. Could we not have destroyed you at any time if we had wanted to? With a crippled ship, were you not at our mercy here if we had evil plans? Will you men of Earth never learn to cast doubt and suspicion aside?"

"I'm not a man of Earth," Ben said doggedly. "I'm a Spacer, and it is hard to cast doubt and suspicion aside."

A peal of musical laughter sounded in Ben's ears. "Not a man of Earth? Indeed! And can you live in space without the protection of your suit? Without oxygen to breathe? Without heat, without moisture?"

"No," Ben said.

The laughter came again. "I thought not. You must carry Earth with you wherever you go, yet you claim to be a man of space! Come with me now and you will learn the difference between men of Earth like yourself and men of space."

The creature turned and started down the rubble-strewn path. Ben looked at Tom and Joyce for a moment, then started after the creature. The Barrons followed single file. It was difficult going; the creature was nimble and his pace was swift. But presently they encircled another great spur of rock and saw a crude stairway hewn down the rock wall into a cavern. Above them a huge black cliff seemed to rise smooth and gleaming. It was only then that Ben realized that the cavern was a metal hatchway, and that the gleaming cliff was the hull of a ship so huge it seemed to extend from horizon to horizon.

It was the phantom ship they had encountered before. Now it was visible and at rest, yet even now the outlines were slightly indistinct. Their elfin guide was making his way down to the hatchway, and moments later Ben and his companions were inside the ship.

Slowly the hatch clanged shut behind them.

For a moment Ben stopped, trying to adjust his eyes to the dim light inside the ship. They were standing in a huge hallway lighted with luminous poles, with shops and drydocks extending as far as they could see on either side of them. On all sides there were small blue-gray creatures hard at work, hundreds upon hundreds of them. In the drydocks Ben could see a dozen smaller ships swarming with elfin workmen, and across the room showers of sparks flew up from a dozen welding torches. The air was filled with the din of metal on metal; there was hammering and banging, and the whine of winches and the rumbling of overhead cranes carrying crews up and down the hulls of the ships.

The workmen paused as they moved down the center corridor, regarding them curiously with their strange empty blue eyes. Ahead, their guide hurried along as the corridor became a catwalk overlooking huge banks of computers and communications equipment. They passed another area where workmen were posting signals on a vast space map, moving swiftly as powerful radar transmitters swept information into their hands.

For all the hugeness of the ship, Ben Trefon had the curious sensation that he was in a dream world, a giant among elves, towering head and shoulders above the creatures that crowded around them as they passed. Yet from the way these creatures stood and from the expressions on their wizened faces, Ben wondered who the giants were, after all. There was nothing he could pinpoint, but could feel the enormous power of these people, a power that could obliterate him instantly if it were ever to be activated, yet a power which was dormant rather than active. There was no sign of hostility here; indeed, these creatures were regarding him with eagerness and expectation. All about him, whispering wordlessly in his ear, Ben could feel the wave of excitement growing as though a mighty bowstring were being pulled back until it was ready to snap.

It was an uncanny feeling, and a glance at Tom and Joyce's puzzled faces told Ben that they could feel it too. But there was no time to stop and try to catch distinct impressions. Their escort turned suddenly down a side corridor and ushered them into a small room that looked surprisingly like the library of a Spacer home on Mars. One wall of the room was covered with a bank of instruments; another side held a huge store of microfilm spools and magnetic tapes. As they entered the room their eyes were drawn to the diminutive gray figure at a desk at the far side.

He was a creature like the others, but somehow he looked older, and his shoulders were bent as though he were carrying an enormous weight. He rose as the door closed behind them, and the creature who had escorted them hurried forward to greet him.

And once again Ben heard the musical voice in his ear saying, "Greetings, brother. They have come to us at last, even as you predicted."

Across the room the creature stirred slightly, turning smoky blue eyes upon them for so long that Ben felt himself getting dizzy staring at them. Then the creature made another move, and a deeper voice echoed in Ben's ears. "You have come a long way, both in time and in space," the Elder was saying. "You must be tired and hungry, perhaps confused."

"We're confused, all right," Ben said sharply. "Who are you people? Where do you come from, and what are you doing here?"

"We are dwellers of the Rings, just as you are," the voice came back gently. "And we have known your people well, in times past. The belt of power has been our avenue of contact. Now you must let me examine the one you wear." The voice hesitated. "This chamber is pressurized and supplied with your oxygen needs. You may safely remove your suits."

Stepping out of the heavy pressure suit, Ben loosened the black web belt from his waist. The capsule was still vibrating like a thing alive. When the creature reached out for it, their fingers touched for an instant, and Ben felt a tingle much like a slight electric shock. But the creature was slipping the capsule from the webbing, staring at it minutely.

He examined it for a long time in silence. Then he looked up at Ben. "So Ivan Trefon is really dead in this senseless war of yours," the voice said sadly. "I had hoped to the last that our information might be wrong, that such a man had not really been wasted so tragically. But you are now wearing the belt that he wore."

"I'm his son," Ben said. "But my father never spoke of you."

"I know. Your father was a man of honor and integrity. He kept the pledge of silence he made, for he knew that the time had not come to speak of us. In all the centuries that we have counseled with men of Earth it has never been time. But now perhaps it must become time, whether the time is right or not." The creature looked straight at Ben Trefon. "Your war with the Earth-dwelling men must end before it is too late. Already it has gone too far for simple means, but this time we cannot intervene openly. We intervened once before, against our judgment, and the results were tragic. This time only you can intervene for yourselves."

Ben saw the puzzled frowns on the Barrons' faces. "We don't understand," he told the creature. "You seem to know so much about us, and we know nothing about you."

"How we know is not important now," the creature replied. "*What* we know is urgently important. We know that you dwellers in space still do not realize the determination of your Earth brothers to destroy you. We know that many Spacers have withdrawn to their last battlement, their Central asteroid, and that the remaining forces have gathered to prepare a disastrous counterattack on Earth itself. Should Asteroid Central fall, the trigger would be pulled and a planetary holocaust would result." The creature hesitated. "We cannot read the future. We can only predict on the basis of long and bitter experience. Should your war be pursued to its end, the odds are four to one that all human life in the solar system will be obliterated, that the spark will be extinguished once and for all. And that cannot be permitted to happen."

"But that's not possible!" Tom Barron cried. "You talk as if we were children."

"This is a war of children," the creature returned sharply. "Only children would slaughter each other out of ignorance and fear. Only children would fail again and again to learn the lessons of their foolishness, and stubbornly, blindly persist in their childishness. Don't speak to me about children, I know what children you are. But I also know the greatness you could achieve if you would only put away childish things."

They stood silent under the rebuke. Behind the creature's words Ben could sense a powerful wave of exasperation and anger mixed with concern, the exasperation and concern of an adult for a willful and recalcitrant child, mixed with apprehension and sorrow. For the first time Ben began to see some connection between these strange creatures and the events that had been happening. Pieces of the puzzle suddenly began to fit. He looked up at the little gray figure across the room. "You people are not from Earth," he said. "You don't come from any place in the solar system, do you?"

"Of course not," the creature replied.

"Then who are you? Why do you care what happens to us in our wars?"

"Because that is our purpose here: to care. We have watched your planet for millennia, since the first spark of intelligence flared up in your people, and we have watched that spark grow into the raging fire it is today. Our job is to keep that fire alive until you cease being children and learn how to control it yourselves, until you learn how to *use* it. Then our work here will be done, if you have not destroyed yourselves in your childishness before you can mature. But one of your own people can tell you about us better than I can. I believe that your father left you something else as well as the belt of power, did he not?"

"The tape," Tom Barron said.

"Yes, there was a tape," Ben said. "A mauki chant, but we couldn't understand it."

"Let me see the tape" the creature said.

Ben drew the spool from an inner pocket and handed it over. The creature went to a player at the side of the room, placed the tape in the slot and adjusted the controls.

"It won't be any good," Ben said. "It's in a language none of us understands."

The tiny gray creature smiled. "Who knows?" he said. "Perhaps you will understand it now. Perhaps that in itself will help you understand why we are here."

For a moment there was no sound in the room but the swish-swish of the tape in the player, Then, suddenly, the room was flooded with music. It was the same music that Ben and Tom had heard from the player in the vault below the House of Trefon, the same measured rhythms, the same woman's haunting voice, the same refrain they had heard before. Even the words were the same, words which had seemed familiar but not quite understandable before, as if they were words of a subtly different tongue.

But now, incredibly, the meaning of the words became clear. Ben stared at the frayed tape going through the player, heard the same scratchy defects from repeated replaying as he had heard before, but now the mauki's chant was understandable, unmistakable in its meaning.

Like so many of the mauki chants Ben had heard, this was a story set to music. Like those other chants, it dealt with times and places and great events, but this story was utterly strange to Ben Trefon. He listened, and the Barrons listened too, their faces reflecting the increasing wonder in their minds as the story unfolded.

It was the story of a people, but not of human people. They were similar to men in many ways, with the loves and hates and fears of men, but a people far older and greater and more powerful than men had ever dreamed of being. These people had been living for untold ages at the time when Earth and her sun were no more than motes of dust in the emptiness of space between the galaxies. Already then these people had been engaged for eons in an endless, patient search through the vast reaches of the universe. Where they had come from and why and how they had first begun to roam the galaxies even they themselves did not know . . . but they did know that they had a purpose to fulfill, a purpose that spanned all space and extended through all time. And that purpose was to search out, wherever it might be, with infinite patience and perseverance, a certain tiny flame that they knew flickered up from time to time in new galaxies and old across the firmament.

They were called the Searchers, and their dedication to their goal exceeded understanding. There was no time too long to wait, no distance too far to travel, if there was hope that their search might finally lead once again to another source of precious flame they sought. They did not know what that flame was, nor how it came about, nor why it occurred when it did, but they knew full well the incredible, unthinkable power for good or for evil that it signified. And they knew that there was nothing more rare and wonderful in all the universe than this tiny flame whenever it appeared anew: the flame of intelligence flaring up in a race of creatures evolving here or there across the galaxies, with the reason and compassion and strength that always accompanied it.

Time and again the Searchers discovered the flame of intelligence burning brightly on remote planets of remote stars; each new discovery was a time for rejoicing, for then once again the real work of the Searchers could begin. Most intelligent races were planet-born and star-bound. Without aid they would arise, and flourish, and die within the boundaries of their own solar systems, perhaps sensing that other intelligences existed elsewhere in the universe, but unable to reach across the immensities of interstellar space to contact them. Some, more advanced than others, even sensed that their intelligence, in itself, was incomplete, that its real potentials could never possibly be realized without joining with other intelligences across the starways. And for them the tragedy was even greater if they could not find a way to reach from galaxy to galaxy.

But the Searchers were not planet-born, and their lives were not bounded by the time limits of racial history. Geological ages for them were the same as minutes on their time scale; they alone could take the time to search out intelligence wherever it might arise, and nurse it to maturity, and draw it into contact with the great community of intelligent races that grew and flourished in the universe of life. For the Searchers it was a sacred trust that they could not and would not relinquish.

There had been a time when a group of Searchers, traveling with incredible power through the depths of space, had sensed the tiny flame of intelligence flaring up in a race of creatures living on the third planet of a medium-sized main-sequence star situated far out on one of the arms of an immense spiral galaxy. How the Searchers had sensed its presence no one could say; it was enough that they knew it was there, and with excitement and joy plans were made for contact. But contact was approached with caution as the Searchers landed upon the planet where the flame was burning. Long experience had taught them to observe and assess a new intelligence first in secrecy and silence, for raw intelligence without the temper of maturity could do immeasureable harm if contacted too soon. Almost at once the Searchers knew that a flaw was present here, a flaw they had encountered countless times before.

There was intelligence among these creatures who called themselves men. There was reason among them, there was an enormous vigor and curiosity, but their intelligence was raw and uncontrolled. The Searchers had seen the flaw in other races before; these men themselves had words to describe the flaw that crippled them. Like children who had never grown up, their intelligence lacked maturity and compassion. They were only beginning to grasp the difference between themselves and the unintelligent creatures that lived and died around them. Their potential was enormous; the things that they might one day accomplish in a community of intelligent races were staggering, but they were not yet ready for even a suspicion that they might have such potential, for they still thought and acted and behaved as children.

It was a sinister flaw, a grave impediment. The Searchers knew that some intelligent races had never learned to overcome it. Some had lived out their racial history in ignorance of what they might become simply because they had never grown up enough to be told. And it was a flaw which had to be overcome before contact with other races could be permitted.

For a childish intelligence could never cope with the powers that contact would provide them. A race of intelligent children would never contribute. It would only exploit. Without maturity, this intelligent race of men was incredibly dangerous, far too dangerous to entrust with knowledge it would be unable to control.

It was tragic, but simple. A child could not be handed a loaded gun.

So the Searchers waited. They had first come to Earth in a time of empire, and they watched in silent horror as great cities arose from the labor of peasants, tyrants bludgeoned their way to power, soldiers marched and slavery flourished. They waited patiently as men struggled and fought among themselves, as children do, watching hopefully for the first signs of maturity to appear. Over the centuries, bit by bit, they began to hope that their patience might ultimately be rewarded.

In the dimly lighted room the song of the mauki paused, and the music changed subtly. Ben shook his head, only half comprehending what he was hearing. The Barrons seemed equally wonder-struck. It was as if something was drawing out their minds and painting a picture for them through other eyes, a picture of their own people that they had never seen before. A thousand questions burst into Ben's mind, but there was no chance to ask them, for the mauki's song continued, an incredible song, yet a song so compelling that it defied disbelief.

True to their purpose, the Searchers had waited, watching the painful progress of this race of intelligent creatures called men. They listened to the clank of metal armor and smelled the sweaty leather of the Roman armies as they marched north into Gaul. They heard the thundering hoofbeats of the invading hordes from the East, and watched the crumbling of the mighty empire that had been Rome. Throughout the dark centuries that followed they watched and waited, occasionally reaching out for momentary contact with one man or another. Bit by bit their presence became known in the physical form they had chosen to use on Earth, and legends grew up among men, folk stories of elves and trolls and other creatures of the middle world, living on Earth with men but hidden from men's senses unless they chose to be revealed.

With quickening excitement the Searchers witnessed the blossoming of intelligence as the Middle Ages drew to a close and men discovered science and began systematically to explore their own minds and the physical world that lay about them. The signs of maturity began to gather; the capability was there. Soon, the Searchers were saying to each other, soon the time for contact would arrive.

Then, before their eyes, the variable appeared that the Searchers had been dreading. Just as a child grows rapidly in one way and remains a child in others, these men began moving swiftly with their new-found knowledge of science, and lagging in other areas. In rapid succession two terrible wars broke out, driving Earth technology before them even as humanity was forgotten. The day came when the Searchers saw an enormous bomb explode over an Earth city and form the dreadful mushroom cloud of atomic holocaust, and they knew that the turning point had been reached. They knew men now held the key to utter self-destruction. These children had fashioned their own gun and turned it upon themselves as the struggle between the perpetual childhood of slavery and the mature ideal of free individuals in a free society went on.

No one could choose for them as men continued striving to resolve that struggle. Leaping forward, they learned to leave their planet and explore their solar system, landing outposts of men on Earth's moon, on Mars, on Venus. Slowly the struggle between slavery and freedom intensified, building up to a frightful war of nuclear weapons fought on Earth and in space alike, and slowly that war became probable, and then inevitable, and the Searchers at last were faced with a terrible choice: either to intervene or to allow these creatures to destroy themselves before their childhood ended.

Right or wrong, the Searchers chose to intervene.

It was an unthinkable choice for these observers from the stars, for bitter experience had told them that intervention in itself could precipitate disaster. But the alternative was equally unthinkable. Nuclear wars in other places and in other times had wiped life from the faces of planets. Intelligent races, flaring with such promise as these men, had been utterly destroyed. Intervention was considered the lesser of the evils, and cautious contacts were made with certain key humans, certain mature men, among the brave crews manning the opposing garrisons in space. By using the belts of power to contact certain men, the Searchers had revealed themselves, and on the very eve of the Great War, had drawn from these men their agreement to protect their race from itself by withholding fire when the war began.

As a result, it was a small war instead of a large one. The planet Earth was injured, but the race was not destroyed. Yet the intervention of the Searchers had proven a two-edged sword which even they could not control, and out of the Great War a new division had grown up to split men into warring factions. Hatred and spite and ignorance still outweighed maturity in the minds of men. The forces in space were driven into exile there by their planet-bound brothers. Instead of healing the breach, time opened it wider as the necessities of survival threw fuel on the fire that raged between Earthmen and Spacers.

Until now, once again, a war of obliteration had begun, and the Searchers knew that somehow, once again, they were forced to intervene.

At first it semed like a fairy story, a fantastic tale without any real connection with the lives of Spacers and Earthmen and no relation to the war that was now being fought. But now, as the mauki's voice faded into silence and Ben looked across at Tom Barron's sober face, he knew that they had been hearing no fantasy. They had been hearing plain history, a history none of them had ever heard before, but history nonetheless.

And now bits and pieces of the story began to fit together with other things Ben had known but had never understood. After that first intervention, with its tragic aftermath of Spacer exile, the Searchers had withdrawn, realizing that no solution had been found after all. But they maintained contact from time to time with certain representatives of the Spacer clan. Great care was taken to select men with more than usual maturity for contact, in hopes that through their leadership some way to repair the rift with Earthmen might be found.

Ivan Trefon had been one of their contacts. His father before him had been entrusted with one of the belts of power, to enable him to contact the Searchers should contact be necessary, and to allow the Searchers to contact him. And now Ben began to understand the real work his father had been doing, as a leader of the Spacers and as a member of the Council. Guided and directed by the Searchers, Ivan Trefon had spent his life working to bring peace between Earthmen and Spacers. Somehow he too had captured the vision the Searchers had brought with them: a vision of the enormous power for good that lay dormant in human intelligence if only the maturity could be found to control it. Ivan Trefon's dedication had been fierce and unceasing, yet before his eyes he had seen the clouds of obliterative war gather, goaded on by hate and fear and ignorance.

It was no wonder, Ben thought, that his father had appeared so defeated and weary at the time of Ben's last visit to the house on Mars.

But this time the Searchers themselves were helpless, for all their power. The Great War had appeared a disastrous accident, permitted to occur only through ignorance on the part of men, and the Searchers had decided against their better judgment to intervene to stop it. But now the same pattern seemed about to be repeated; nothing had been learned the first time, and these men of Earth had come no closer to the end of childishness than before. The Searchers now faced the bitter fact that these children could not be forced into maturity. If they were to overcome their flaw, it must be done under their own power. Again and again the Searchers had met to consider new intervention, and again and again the same answer had been reached. Men *could* leave childishness behind; the Spacer leaders had proven that in refusing to allow the Great War to obliterate the race. And if men could grow to maturity and would not, further intervention would be useless. If Earthmen and Spacers now were bent upon destruction, it was within their power; this time men themselves must make the choice.

Ben Trefon's eyes caught the misty blue eyes of his host. "You mean that you refuse to intervene this time," he said.

"We have done all that we can," the Searcher's voice said in Ben's ear.

"But how could this war threaten the entire race?" Ben said. "Spacers might be wiped out, yes, but Earth itself would remain."

"If that were true, we would never have drawn you into contact," the Searcher said. "But your own Spacer fleet command has not been idle. Asteroid Central is under siege, but Spacer ships unable to return there have been massing around Outpost 3 for days, resisting every Earth attempt to disband them. That Spacer fleet has warheads sufficient to reduce Earth to a cinder, should they be launched effectively at close range. And certain of the fleet leaders have prepared a counterattack." The little creature eyed Ben Trefon sadly. "Your people have never before been vindictive," he said. "But after the desolation of Mars by Earth ships, there is a spirit of revenge abroad among Spacers. If so much as a single shell from an Earth ship should penetrate the Maze and strike Asteroid Central, a fleet of Spacer ships will depart instantly from Outpost 3, to strike a devastating counter-blow at Earth herself. Spurred by vengeance, there will be no stopping that fleet if it leaves. And our calculations indicate that no living thing will be left on Earth should your warheads be released."

There was a long silence. Then Joyce Barron turned to the tiny creature across the room. "This is true, what you say?"

"We have vision-proof ships observing every sector in the Rings. I am speaking the truth."

"But not the whole truth," Joyce said. "You claim that you will not intervene, and yet right now in this room you are intervening by drawing us into contact. Is that not true?"

Their host hesitated a fraction of a second. "Your reasoning is sound, of course. We have already intervened, to this extent. But a different kind of intervention than before."

"Then why did you bring us here?" the girl cried. "You must have had a reason. Why us? Why not other Earthmen and other Spacers?"

"Because we are still hoping that this disaster may be stopped," the Searcher said, "and already you—the three of you—have taken the first critical step to stop it."

They stared at the tiny elfin creature, and then at each other as the Searcher continued.

"You may be the only three humans alive who can succeed where we have failed."

Hours later, after they had been escorted out of the Searchers' ship, back through the cleft in the rock and into Ben Trefon's little S-80, the three friends still were not certain that they had fully understood the responsibility that had suddenly fallen on their shoulders. Their memory of the encounter with the Searchers already had taken on a dreamlike quality, and as they sat and talked through the long hours, neither Ben nor the Barrons could be entirely certain that the encounter had not been a strange kind of delusion that they had shared together.

The Searchers were gone. Their escort had turned away from them at the entrance hatch to the S-80, and then vanished as though a light had been switched out. The tools Ben and Tom had left out were still where they had dropped them when they first became alarmed about Joyce's disappearance, and everything since seemed slightly blurry in their memories.

And yet they all remembered quite clearly the haunting

strains of the mauki chant and the strange story it had told, preserved for them on the ancient tape.

"I just don't understand," Joyce said when they were back in the ship with the hatch closed behind them. "You and Tom had listened to that tape before, and couldn't understand it. How did we understand it in there?"

"It was being translated for us," Ben said. "There's no other explanation. We were hearing it through the Searchers' ears. And yet we weren't reading their minds. I'm sure that the tape was necessary for us to understand at all."

Tom stuck his hands in his pockets. "Remember what he said before he started playing it—that hearing it would demonstrate something to us. Maybe he was trying to show us what two intelligent races in co-operation could do that neither could do alone."

Ben nodded. "I thought of that. There never has been any real success in our scientists' attempts to study extrasensory perception. It has always seemed as if men have had half a talent, and were missing the other half, somehow. And if another race of creatures somewhere had the other half—" He paused, shaking his head. "It could mean almost anything. Our bodies are limited by the temperatures and environments we can survive, but our minds aren't. Even the speed-of-light barrier to star travel might fall away, if another intelligent race could help us away from our bodily limitations. Maybe our intelligence, here in our solar system, is just a tiny piece in a huge puzzle."

"But what did the Searcher mean about stopping the war?" Joyce said. "He made it seem that we were the only ones who could hope to do anything."

"Don't you see?" Tom said excitedly. "Where else have Earthmen and Spacers joined hands and learned the truth about each other? Nowhere else. Yet you and I and Ben know that this war is pointless folly. There isn't a single valid reason for it, if each side knew the truth about the other. And that was what the Searchers were trying to tell us, that somehow we have to tell both sides the *truth* and make them believe it just as we do."

"It sounds good," Ben said, "but how? I don't have any power among my people, even if I could get to Asteroid Central, and that would mean running the Maze right under the nose of five hundred Earth ships. And as for you convincing your people—oh, it's hopeless. Who would believe us? How could we tell them a story like this and get anybody even to *listen?*"

"You already know the answer to that," Joyce Barron said quietly. "We can get people to listen just the way the Searchers got us to listen."

Ben frowned. "I don't follow you."

"There was a ship that came back from a reprisal raid, years ago," Joyce said. "An Earth ship, one of the 'pirates' you spoke of. They kidnaped a mauki and her five-year-old boy, and then destroyed the boy and tried to get the mauki back home. It didn't work; they fell into a trap, and a Spacer ship boarded them and recaptured the mauki. But the reason they were trapped was because the mauki was singing."

Ben looked skeptical. "How could *that* have been a trap?"

"You're used to mauki chants. You've heard them all your life, and still you stop and listen, don't you?"

"Well, I suppose I do."

"Yes. And when that woman in that ship began to sing, every crewman stopped what he was doing to listen."

They stared at her in silence. Then Ben said, "She's got it, Tom. She's got the answer. If we can find a way to put it to work in time."

9 THE MAZE

BIT BY BIT, then, a plan evolved from their council of war. It was a slender thread to hang upon, but at least it was a beginning. Time after time Ben shook his head hopelessly and they nearly discarded the whole idea; it was almost suicidally risky, and even should the first steps succeed, there was no real hope that it would work when the chips were really down. It would be a desperation move, and there would be no turning back once they had started.

But time after time they came back to face the plain facts: feeble as it might be, it was the only conceivable plan that could work. Already things had moved too far and too fast. There would be no time for negotiating, no time to try a little at a time to get across to people on Earth and in space the awful implications of this war. It had to be done swiftly and surely, in terms that nobody could possibly misunderstand.

"We'll only have one chance," Tom said gloomily, looking up at Ben and his sister. "We've got to be certain it's worth the risk."

Ben nodded. "It's worth it. My father never stopped to worry about the risk. That was why he had a belt to wear."

"Then let's get moving. There isn't time to waste."

The first impediment was staring them in the face already. The ship was still disabled. With renewed energy Tom and Ben tackled the repair work again, and now Joyce worked with them, driven by the same sense of urgency the others felt. During rest periods they talked, filling in details of the plan as best they could. It seemed incredible to them now that they had once mistrusted each other; now they were haunted by only one fear: that disaster might strike before they could get moving, that they might put their plan into action only to discover that they were too late.

But on the third day after their encounter with the Searchers, news came from an unexpected direction. The ship's radar picked up a signal, revealed a small ship moving at a tangent in toward the asteroid, and Ben's tentative recognition signal brought a jubilant response. A few moments later another Spacer S-80 was landing, piloted by a tall, white-haired man who greeted Ben with a hearty embrace as soon as he saw who he was.

It was Elmo Peterson, chief mechanic of the House of Trefon before the raid on the Earth ships.

The reunion was a happy one, Elmo had been one of the men who had broken free from the planet, carrying a cruiserfull of refugees with him, when the raid had begun. Once they had been safely interned on one of the outposts he had picked up an S-80, and now was cruising the Rings for stragglers, directing them on to Outpost 3 to join the fleet that was gathering there.

"But what about Asteroid Central?" Ben wanted to know.

"It's touch-and-go," the white-haired Spacer said. "The snakes can't break through the Maze, but they have ships in there so thick a frontal assault against them wouldn't stand a chance. Nobody would have believed they could have manned such a fleet, but they have. We've lost three squadrons that have hit them trying to break the siege. Another attempt would just be suicide. So we're working out an alternative."

"You mean an assault on Earth itself," Ben said.

The big man gave Ben a sharp look. "As a matter of fact, that's the plan. Get them at the roots. They have everything they own tied up in this armada out here, with only the shakiest defenses back home. If they can't break the Maze, they can still starve us out of Central sooner or later. So while they're sitting there waiting for something to happen, we plan to move in on their home ground."

Ben nodded. "And what do you plan to do when you get there?"

"Play the game by *their* rules," Peterson said. "You saw what they did to Mars. Well, Mars is going to look like paradise when we get through with the planet Earth. Every factory, every city, every storage dump, every road junction —they don't realize how many ships we will have *outside* Central when all the stragglers are in. We're still rounding up ships heading in from Ganymede and Europa and Titan. When we move those ships in against Earth, our friends out here aren't going to have any place to go home to." The big Spacer eyed the Barrons with distaste, then looked back at Ben. "We'll want you and your ship with us, naturally. But we don't have any use for this pair."

Ben hesitated. It was an unexpected complication, and a

tough one to get around. "What does the command on Central have to say about this?" he asked cautiously.

Elmo Peterson spread his hands. "They don't know about it. The snakes have cut off communication completely; we haven't gotten a message through for days."

"And who's commanding your fleet?"

"Tommy Whisk."

"You mean he's going along with this plan?" Ben asked. astonished.

"Not because he likes it, you can bet on that," Elmo said. "You know Tommy Whisk. But now even he thinks it has to be done. We've got to break this siege somehow."

Ben nodded, thinking furiously. He had known Tommy Whisk from years before, when he had been one of Ivan Trefon's closest friends on the Spacer Council. It was incredible that the elderly Navajo would be a party to a mass attack on Earth unless he truly believed it was a last desperate hope to break the siege. On the Spacer birth rolls Thomas Manywhisker was listed as one of a long line of wise Spacer leaders, and he was known to retain much of the ancient stolidity, patience, and perseverance that had always been so characteristic of his people.

And if Tommy Whisk were in command of the outlying Spacer fleet, he would welcome any approach to a peaceful end of the war. Ben struck his palm with his fist. "Look," he said to Elmo. "The Council on Asteroid Central would want to know before any raiding fleet goes off half-cocked."

"Yes, if they could be told. But how? Tommy has tried every way imaginable to get word through. There just isn't time left to try any more."

"But suppose there *was* a way," Ben said.

"Tommy would surely want to know it."

"All right," Ben said. "Help me get this crate spaceworthy again, and I'll get word to Asteroid Central."

Elmo blinked at him. "By magic, maybe?"

"Not quite. I'll run the blockade."

"That's no good. It's been tried."

"I've got a way to make it work. And I won't bring any Earth ship through with me, either. Give me twenty-four hours and I'll have word back to you from the Council."

The big Spacer shook his head. "Ben, you're talking about a suicide run. You wouldn't stand a chance. And, anyway, Tommy's orders were specific. I'm supposed to bring back any Spacer I run into to help build up the fleet."

"I think this is more important," Ben said. "I think Tommy

would agree." He hesitated a minute, then took the plunge. "Go back and give him a message from me. Tell him I have my father's belt. I think he'll understand. Tell him to give me twenty-four hours. If he hasn't had word direct from Asteroid Central by then, tell him to go ahead. Because if I can't do it in twenty-four hours, he'll know it can't be done."

Deep in the hold of the little S-80 the engines were throbbing once again, sending a barely palpable vibration through the whole ship. At the controls Ben Trefon made an occasional adjustment in course, with an uneasy eye on the radar screen, trying to fight down the panic that kept struggling for control, ever since he had moved away from the comparative safety of the asteroid.

Elmo Peterson had been hard to convince, but Ben had convinced him finally. Only after Ben had assured him and reassured him that he would be able to run the blockade successfully had the big Spacer reluctantly agreed to go along with Ben's plan. Ultimately it was the fact that Ben was Ivan Trefon's son that convinced him; Elmo Peterson had seen Ben's father accomplish many things in the past that were supposed to be impossible until he proved by doing them that they weren't. Even then Elmo had wanted to take the Barrons back to the Spacer fleet with him, fearing for Ben's safety with them aboard. But at last Ben had convinced him that their threat was outweighed by their possible usefulness as hostages in running the blockade, and Elmo departed with his message for Tommy Whisk.

But now Ben was beginning to wish he had not been carried away. Convincing Elmo was easy. Convincing himself was another story, because he knew too well that he had no magic to help him move through the blockade and in to Asteroid Central safe from attack.

All he had to help him was a black web belt around his waist. When they had first developed their plan, it had depended on the belt. The Searchers would surely be watching what they did, and the capsule in the belt was obviously a means of communication and control. If the Searchers would respond with the help Ben needed when he needed it, as they had promised they would, he knew he could run the blockade successfully. If the Searchers would not respond, everything would be lost.

But when they had tried to find the Searchers to tell them the plan, after Elmo Peterson had departed, they were nowhere to be found. The cleft in the rock was gone, and there was no sign of the great phantom ship. Except for one thing, Ben might have been convinced the Searchers were only a figment of his imagination, so completely had they disappeared. That one thing was the belt, with the capsule that still was vibrating ever so faintly against Ben's side.

Now that they were committed, and had embarked on the plan, all the questions they had raised before returned to plague them. And with the disappearance of the Searchers, Ben's doubts redoubled. For unless the belt could produce help, they were indeed on a suicide run. Ben was certain, from Elmo's reports and his own knowledge of space logistics, that no ordinary space ship could hope to run the blockade and sneak into the Maze to the stronghold in the center without taking an enemy shell broadside. Only by becoming a phantom ship, like the ship of the Searchers themselves, could he hope to run the gauntlet successfully.

Out of the corner of his eye Ben saw a faint blip appear and fade on the radar screen. On the next cycle the signal was stronger, and the capsule at his belt began vibrating a little more strongly. Ben motioned Tom to the 'scope, and a moment later Tom nodded and breathed a sigh of relief. "They're there," he said. "Just a little behind us, but there. They have their vision screen down; I can see the ship."

"Then they must realize what we're going to try to do," Ben said. He grinned at his companion, some of the tension easing. "Who knows but we might make it yet?"

All three of them were at the control panel now as the little ship carried them through the blackness toward the area where Asteroid Central would soon be passing in its orbit, surrounded by the great armada that held it in siege. Ben turned controls over to Tom while he ate a few bites of the meal Joyce had prepared, then lay down for an hour's rest before resuming his vigil. Sleep was impossible, but he forced his tense muscles to relax. Presently he did doze, only to be awakened by Tom shaking his injured shoulder.

"Better take over," Tom said. "I think we've just spotted the outside ring of the blockade."

Back at control, Ben stared through the 'scope, scanning the segment of space ahead for signs of the gathering of Earth ships. Somewhere up there was the great Central asteroid, but neither Ben nor Tom could see it yet in the 'scope, nor could they see the multitude of tiny rocks and debris whirling about it to form the dense protective screen of the Maze. But the 'scope did pick up the faint shadow of a ship up ahead, and then another and another . . . the first circle of blockading Earth ships that held Asteroid Central trapped and helpless.

Carefully, Ben blacked out the ship's lights and altered the course slightly, bringing the S-80 into the precise direction and orbital speed necessary to move parallel to the Central asteroid. Then, ever so slowly, he began edging the ship in toward the first circle of besieging ships he knew lay waiting.

In the darkness of the cabin, the tension became almost unbearable. More and more signals appeared on the radar screen—a dozen ships, two dozen. Still Ben edged in closer to them. Once the blockade was run, the Maze would be no problem, with the key recorded in special memory circuits in the ship's computer. Then there would only be the danger of some Earth ship following him through. But with the intervening ships in a tightly drawn circle around the asteroid, the Maze seemed a million miles away.

A moment later Tom said, "There! I can see the asteroid now. And it looks like a swarm of bees are around it."

"That's right," Ben said. "If only I can sneak in close enough to make a run for it, we'll be plenty happy to have that swarm of bees for protection."

"But it looks like we're moving right through the blockade," Tom said, looking at the radar screen.

"Don't fool yourself. Watch the pattern there for a moment."

The shift in the pattern was subtle, but it was there. The little S-80 had moved into the first ring of ships without opposition. But now the ships behind them were beginning to close together, until Earth ships were on all sides of them. Tom watched incredulously. "Do you suppose they haven't spotted us?" he asked.

"Oh, they've spotted us all right."

"Then why don't they challenge us?"

"There's the reason," Ben said, pointing to the screen. "Those two big fellows moving in on us. They're not sure we're Spacer yet. They want us well covered before they flush us, just in case we are. Meanwhile they're trying to make up their minds what's going on."

Suddenly there was a burst of static from the radio speaker, and then a sharp challenge. "You, there, moving in the pattern. Strike your engines and identify yourself."

"Sorry, I'm drifting," Ben snapped back into the microphone. "I'm trying to correct for my drift." He let the little ship ease deeper into the pattern of blockade ships.

There was a moment of hesitation. Then the challenger's

voice came through again. "Identify yourself and tell me what's wrong."

"Something's wrong with one of my gyros," Ben replied.

"What ship are you? And who's in command?" The voice was imperative now. "Mister, you're warned. If you don't kill your engines and identify yourself you're going to be hit."

The two approaching ships were quite close now on the screen. Suddenly there was a flash from the forward tubes of the closest ship and a missile streaked toward them. "I guess that's the end of their patience," Ben said to Tom. "They're firing now. Hold tight." In the same breath he slammed down the four main drive switches. The tiny ship suddenly leaped forward like a frightened deer, heading straight for the center of the blockade.

The effect on the approaching ships was electrifying. Before, there had been caution and suspicion; now there was certainty. They knew an enemy was in their midst. Their radar told them it was a single ship moving in from outside, and its action left no doubt of its intent. This was no force attacking the blockading ships. This was a blockade runner, a straggler from the Spacer fleet making a desperate run for the Maze that surrounded Asteroid Central.

Now the radio was blaring a raucous alarm, and searchlight beams pierced the blackness from a dozen surrounding ships, probing with fingers of light to pick up the intruder. On the tracking screen Ben could see that the ships ahead were closing ranks sharply, and other ships were moving above and below him as well. Tom Barron watched the movement on the screen for a moment and turned to Ben in alarm. "You'd better move," he said. "They're closing up the hole behind you."

"Let them," Ben said tersely.

"But they can't miss you if they open fire!"

"What are they going to fire with?" Ben said. "Not contact-detonating shells, that's sure, with all the hardware they have out there. The best they can do is guide their shells until they're sure they're on us, and then detonate manually. And they've got to be able to see us to do that."

Ben broke off, suddenly aware of a powerful vibration at his waist. In the same moment a thought popped into his mind, and he reached a hand forward for the emergency generator switches far to the right on the control panel.

He was already throwing the switches when he realized with a jolt that the thought had not been his own at all.

There was a high-pitched whine from the engine room, and

the lights on the control panel flickered. Behind them, incredibly, something was happening to the two great Earth cruisers which had been bearing down on the little Spacer ship so swiftly. One swerved suddenly and drew back; the other faltered in its course, moving back and forth as if in confusion. At the same time an angry wave of chatter burst forth from the radio.

"Where did he go? Where did he go?"

"Darned thing vanished!"

"What do you mean, vanished? You moved between us to block my view."

"You're the one that's blocking the view, you idiot."

Now the whole defensive movement of the blockading ships was dissolving in confusion. Searchlights beat the darkness in wilder and wilder arcs, and the converging ships began scattering and circling as if their pilots had suddenly gone mad.

"What's happening?" Tom said. "The crazy fools are fumbling all over the place!"

Ben Trefon chuckled, and hit the drive switch, moving swiftly on in toward the Maze. "It's hard to home in on a shadow," he said. "Remember how hard it was to see the Searchers' ship, even when we knew exactly where it was?"

"But we don't have any screening devices!"

"I think we do. Something's hooked into the emergency power circuits, and we didn't touch those circuits when we were repairing. But we were away from the ship for several hours while we were aboard the Searchers' ship."

"You think they installed something?"

"Our friends out there can't see us," Ben replied. "What do you think? There's going to be some tall explaining in blockade headquarters tonight, I'll bet you on that."

Now the blockade was thinning out on the tracking screen, and ahead the great disk of Asteroid Central was clearly visible, with its company of satellite rocks whizzing about it in dizzying confusion. As they approached, a warning signal buzzed on the control panel. "Overloading the generators," Ben said. "Whatever their gadget is, it sucks up power. We'd better try to do without it now." Snapping the emergency switches off again, Ben nosed the little ship into the Maze. "Hold on, now. You're going to have a rough trip."

Deftly he moved the ship into a tangential arc, sliding into the edge of the Maze just as a large asteroid fragment came whirling by, rolling end-over-end. There were half a dozen possible keys to the Maze; Ben chose the avenue he knew best from experience, using the computers to outline his directional changes and maneuvers, but making the fine adjustments by the seat of his pants. Suddenly the ship was surrounded by rapidly whirling rock fragments going in all directions, some coming uncomfortably close, but none quite approaching in collision course. This was no job for a machine, when split-second errors in timing might throw a huge chunk of granite directly in a ship's path. On each orbit, each fragment in the Maze shifted its position infinitesimally; only an alert human brain behind the controls of the ship aided by sharp eyes and reflexes could make the fine corrections necessary, using the computer's key as a guide.

Behind them now the blockading ships had again picked up their position. Three fast pursuit ships broke from formation and headed in after them. There was no time for Ben to keep an eye on them; he needed full concentration to weave his way between the hurtling rocks as he guided the ship deeper in to the Maze. With one arm hooked around a shock bar for support he held on for dear life as he fired side jets and breaking jets. In response, the little ship dodged and darted, dropped and skidded like a thing alive.

"Ben, they're trying to follow you in!" Tom said suddenly.

Ben jerked the ship sideways to avoid a huge rock that had loomed up ahead. Beyond the Maze the Great Central asteroid was looming larger now; it was an enormous temptation to break from the key and try to make a run for it when an opening appeared, but Ben held tight to the plotted course. "They're crazy," he said.

"Maybe so, but they must have tracked you. They're following your course."

"Okay." Once again Ben snapped down the emergency generator switches, heard the whine of the screening devices rise again in his ears. "What now?" he asked after a moment.

"They don't go for this on-again-off-again stuff one bit," Tom said. "One's trying to follow, but the other two are turning back."

For a few seconds Ben turned his eyes to the view screen. The pursuit ship that had chosen to follow was in trouble. Once off the track, there were too many moving fragments to watch at once. In the process of dodging one of the Maze asteroids, the pilot moved his ship directly into the path of another. The ship ricocheted into a third, which tore the whole front out of it, and then bounced from one rock to another, gradually beaten to pieces before their eyes.

It looked for a moment as if the two retreating ships would

make it back, but one made the mistake of running for freedom when it had reached the edge. A huge rock caught it broadside, smashing it into a thousand pieces which were hurled in every direction. The rock continued rolling along, not even budged from its course by the impact.

A moment later Ben Trefon let out a shout of glee. The innermost of the Maze asteroids passed by just ahead of the S-80, and suddenly they were in the clear, with the great landing ports of Asteroid Central stretching out below them. Ben switched off the screening devices once again, and circled in toward the main receiving port. As the little ship hovered on null-gravity for landing, the great hatchways swung open to receive it; after a brief exchange of identification, Ben dropped the ship down into the waiting berth.

Moments later a crowd of jubilant Spacers were greeting him on the landing ramp, pounding his back and hoisting him up on their shoulders to carry him into the stronghold, with the Barrons following under somewhat suspicious guard behind him.

The first step of their mission was accomplished.

10 THE MAUKI CHANT

THERE HAD BEEN a time, in the ages before men came into space, when Asteroid Central was no more than another moderate sized chunk of asteroidal rock, one of thousands like it making their way relentlessly in their orbits around the sun near the center of the Asteroid Belt. It was not a large asteroid, originally. Perhaps a hundred miles in diameter, it had been one of the hundreds of asteroid discoveries that had harried Earth astronomers in the 1800's, so far down the list that it was not even given a name. It had been utterly undistinguished in appearance and size, but it had chanced to lie far enough away from mighty Jupiter, the herdsman of the Rings, to have a relatively stable and reliable orbit, and it was this chance of celestial geography that had first led the Spacers to its ragged surface in the early days of their exile.

They had needed a way-station, far enough away from Earth to be difficult to find, yet close enough for use as a supply dump and storage warehouse. As the years passed it became increasingly important as a communications center, and then as a headquarters, roughly central in location, for the blossoming business and economic life that Spacers were building for themselves with the doors of Earth closed to them.

Slowly, bit by bit, Asteroid Central had been molded to their needs. Controlled murexide bombs stolen from Earth warehouses during raids were used to cut tunnels into the surface of the asteroid to provide pressurized storage and supply areas, and drydocks for the repair of Spacer ships. As methods of mining and smelting iron under space conditions were developed, shipyards were built on Asteroid Central's surface, and the ore from other asteroids provided girders and I-beams to build up more useable areas on the surface. Once the body of the asteroid had been tunneled and honeycombed, structural steel formed the basis for the growth of a great city of steel on the surface, and an industrial center for the Spacers began to grow.

Furnishings were built or stolen from Earth. Laboratory space was built for the Spacer scientists, fabrication shops and other manufacturing facilities were painstakingly built up over the centuries, with each decade bringing new growth to the asteroid-city.

As the years passed, it became more and more clear that the Spacers' exile was not destined to come to an end, that they were doomed to become outcasts in the solar system, with no choice but to provide for their needs as best they could, or die. Throughout all history necessity had spurred men on to incredible accomplishments; it was a tribute to man's greatness, perhaps, that the Spacer culture did not shrivel and die as the vengeful Earthmen who had forced their exile had intended it to do. Instead it had grown and flourished, and in flourishing had become steadily more hateful to the people on Earth as guilt gnawed away at their minds.

And Asteroid Central became a symbol of that growth. Over the centuries the city had developed into the great nerve center of the culture, the main communications center, the major city and the central fortress of the Spacer clan. To Ben Trefon the asteroid city, with its winding commercial concourses, its residential wings, its shops and factories and laboratories, its schools and hospitals, was as familiar as the back of his hand. To Tom and Joyce it seemed like an incredible replica of the great steel cities on Earth that they knew so well, a world they had never dreamed that Spacers could even be acquainted with.

Now they were waiting with Ben outside the great Council chambers somewhere deep in the heart of the asteroid. Already word had spread through the city that the son of Ivan Trefon had run the blockade to bring a message from outside, and was demanding an audience with the commander-in-chief of the Spacer Council himself. But the city's jubilation at Ben's return was quickly tempered first with shock and then with suspicion, for he had not returned to the Spacer stronghold alone.

Instead, he had brought with him two of the enemy the city had been learning to hate so deeply, and he brought them not as prisoners but as friends and envoys, insisting that diplomatic courtesy be shown them.

But the Spacers in Asteroid Central were in no temper for diplomacy. Already the strain of the blockade was showing on their faces. The enormous size and power of the invading fleet from Earth had caught Central unprepared. Even the

Spacer Council had been staggered, and now the people of the city were beaten to quarters, beleaguered in their last stronghold. Faces were haggard and eyes worried; voices were guarded, and throughout the city the unspoken questions hovered in everyone's mind: *How long can we hold out? How can we bring an end to the siege, and what will happen if we fail to break it?*

As they waited for the commander-in-chief to appear, Ben fought down a wave of hopelessness. At the worst he had hoped that his own people would accept his friends at face value, at least be willing to listen. Somewhere a beginning had to be made. Asteroid Central could not survive an endless period of siege. Even if there were food and water enough for years, and some way of fighting down the tension of perpetually waiting without any way of fighting back, every new day brought the threat that one of the blockading ships would find a way through the Maze with a cargo of hydrogen warheads in its hold.

And even if the Spacer fleet outside were to attack Earth itself and thus draw away the blockading ships, the Spacers would ultimately lose. Spurred on by anger and vengefulness, there would be no way for the Spacers to control their attack. It would be easy—too easy—to inadvertently smash all life on the planet surface, with radioactive fallout ultimately whittling away the last remains when the attacking ships had gone. With the genetic flaw the Spacers carried, and without maukis to raise their children, even a victorious Spacer clan would presently die, their victory falling into ashes. At the very best, they could hope only for a few survivors, a human race driven back to savagery and forced to begin again the long climb upward.

These were the prospects, if the Searchers' message could not be broadcast in time. This was the price of ignorance and fear. A great deal was clear to Ben Trefon now that he had never suspected when he joined his raiding party just a few short days before. He knew now that the Earthmen's fear of Spacers was based on superstition and myth. He also knew now that his own people's beliefs about Earthmen were distorted by falsehood, distrust and fear. Yet his own contact during the past few days with Tom and Joyce Barron had demonstrated beyond doubt that Earthmen and Spacers were creatures of the same race, human beings with intelligence and resourcefulness and the potential for maturity that the Searchers had been seeking for so long.

If Earthmen and Spacers could reach out for maturity and

leave their childish war behind, there would be nothing to stop human beings from expanding outward to join civilizations beyond the stars. Ben Trefon and the Barrons had proven that it could be done.

But their knowledge was useless unless men on both sides could be made to understand and believe them. And it seemed that even Ben's own people were not willing to listen.

Across the room a door burst open and the commander-in-chief stalked in from the Council chambers. He was a tall, white-haired man. His hands were calloused, and his brown fatigue shirt was open at the neck. His worn dungarees were smeared with grease, but his crude appearance could not disguise the air of dignity and command he carried about him. Ben Trefon could sense the same suppressed power and strength in this man that he had so often sensed in his father, and the blunt honesty in the commander's pale blue eyes was reassuring.

Ignoring the Barrons, the commander clasped Ben's hand warmly. "Welcome home," he said. "We'd almost lost hope of seeing you again." He noticed Ben wince as he moved his injured shoulder. "As soon as we've got things straightened out here, we'll get you up for X-rays and find out why that shoulder is still bothering you."

"The shoulder's fine," Ben lied. "There won't be time for X-rays. There are more important things to do."

The commander regarded him keenly. "You've done quite a bit already, in case you don't know it. You accomplished the next thing to a miracle when you ran that blockade."

Ben looked at him. "I had some extraordinary help," he said.

For the first time the commander glanced at Tom and Joyce. "You also have an extraordinary cargo. Your prisoners present an unpleasant problem. It's unfortunate you brought them in. Our food supplies are already low and dwindling fast. We simply can't afford to feed prisoners of war."

"These are not prisoners," Ben said. "They're friends."

"I understood that they were impounded on Earth during the raid."

"They were. But since then they have become friends, and should be treated as such. If necessary I'll demand it as my right of booty."

There were tired lines on the commander's face, and an expression of infinite weariness. "My son, we are in a desperate war, and we cannot honor individual demands." He stabbed a finger at the Barrons. "The forces these people represent are doing their utmost to choke us to death, and unless we are more fortunate than we appear to be at the moment, they have good odds of succeeding." He shook his head and turned away. "I'm sorry, but your demand is refused. You do your people a dishonor consorting with enemy aliens in times like these."

"As a Spacer," Ben said doggedly, "I have a right to a hearing before judgment is passed."

Anger flared in the commander's eyes. *"Right?* What right? Who are you to be demanding rights at this time? What do you know about this pair? How do you know they aren't spies, deliberately sent to penetrate this fortress? Friendship, indeed! I will not permit my forces here to be contaminated by contact with a pair of Earth-born snakes, nor with you either, if you've been contaminated."

There was a long silence in the little room. Then Ben said, "My father died on Mars. I saw our house after the Earth ships had gone. I saw the houses of my friends there. Do you really think that I've been *contaminated?"*

The commander glared at him for a long moment. Then he sighed and sank down in a chair behind the desk, covering his eyes with his hands in a gesture of weariness. "I'm sorry," he said at length. "The strain has been great, and anger comes too easily. No, I do not really doubt you. I honored your father above all others when he was alive. I grieve for him and honor him in death, and I honor his son as well. But I simply can't understand you. A third of your people are scattered to the four winds, unable to contact us even by radio. And here your people are reaching the breaking point. If I speak in anger, it is simply because I cannot comprehend the presence of these prisoners under your protection."

"Then let me tell you," Ben said. "In the first place, you are wrong about those outside. You have a fleet armed and ready to launch an attack on Earth itself in hopes of breaking this siege. In the absence of countermanding orders from you, they will move in toward Earth in a matter of hours."

The commander leaped up and gripped Ben's arm. "Is this true?" he cried. "They have enough ships, enough arms? They have leadership?"

Ben nodded. "They are well organized, and Tommy Whisk is in command."

"Ah, Tommy! Good, good! But what are they waiting for?"

"They've given me time to reach you and bring word out to them," Ben said. "And if you allow them to launch that attack, we will have lost everything worth fighting for. They must not be allowed to go."

The commander stared at him. "But why not?"

"Because there is a way to peace," Ben said. "That is what we have come to tell you, if only you will listen."

"You mean another way to beat them and break the siege?"

"I mean an end to the war for Earthman and Spacer alike. Whether it can come about or not depends upon you and upon the commander of the blockading fleet. But most of all, it depends upon a mauki."

The woman was tall and straight, with flowing dark hair and eyes that seemed able to see things that the average human eyes failed to see. At Ben Trefon's insistence she had been summoned from her post at a radar station on the surface of the asteroid city; now she greeted Ben with a questioning smile, and gravely acknowledged the two Earthlings without a word.

"They say they have something to tell us," the commander said angrily, pacing the room for control. "They say it can end the war, and that somehow it involves you. Perhaps you can convince them that words will not break this blockade, nor suddenly change the hearts of the ones who attack us."

The mauki said nothing. She merely looked from Ben to the Barrons and back, and waited. She was not young, Ben thought, but her face was very beautiful; now it held no expression, as if she had suddenly drawn a veil to conceal her thoughts. It was a strange face, not exactly hostile, yet not sympathetic either. For some reason he could not fathom, it made Ben Trefon uneasy to look at her, and he turned away to avoid meeting her eyes.

He had never met the woman before, but he knew her history, and he knew the regard with which she was held among all Spacers. She had long been a leader here, with a place of honor on the Council, and her wisdom had served the Spacers well, even if it sometimes seemed remote from the problems at hand.

Perhaps it was that very remoteness that had always made Spacers stop and listen when she sang.

Her story was well known. Years before she had joined the ranks of the Spacers and borne her husband a son. When the child was five, the father was killed in a mining accident in the Rings, and the woman and her son had gone out alone to the place the accident had happened. On the way their ship was halted by an Earth pirate, and the child had been killed.

Yet when a Spacer ship made contact with the pirate and rescued her, the mauki would not permit the Earth ship to be destroyed.

Exactly why she took such a stand no one ever really knew. Some said that she had lost her reason when the child was destroyed. Others insisted that the ship's drive had been damaged beyond repair during the rescue, and the mauki wanted the Earth crew to suffer a lingering death adrift in space in a ship without power. But most often it was said that she had enchanted the entire crew with her singing, forced them to listen in spite of themselves, and then sent them home with a burden of guilt so overwhelming that they could speak of nothing else as long as they lived.

Whatever the truth, Ben Trefon knew one thing: that this woman could sing. There was not a Spacer alive who had not heard her at one time or another, and her singing carried a power that was beyond words to describe. That was the reason he wanted her here.

And now, with the help of Joyce and Tom Barron, he told her the entire story of the things that had happened since he had left his father on Mars on the eve of the raid. No detail was too small to include, for he knew that somehow the woman had to be made to understand. He told her of the aftermath of the raid, of the heartbreaking landing on Mars, of the ruin of his father's house and the legacy he found waiting for him in the vault. He told her of the black web belt and the ancient tape recording, and then of the strange succession of events that had led to contact with the small gray people with the smoky-blue eyes.

The mauki listened without comment, and the commander, almost in spite of himself, listened too. Ben described the visit to the Searchers' ship, and the seemingly miraculous translation of the tape with the help of the Searchers themselves. Finally, he told them of the message on the tape, and concluded with the Searchers' final warning, and their plea that Earthmen and Spacers somehow find a way to cease their hostilities before the point of no return had been reached, and work together to reach out toward the stars.

When he finished, there was utter silence in the room. Then the commander let out a sigh and turned to Ben. "Do you really mean me to believe that this fantastic story is true?"

"It's true, you can be sure of that."

"And you expect me to believe that these Earth snakes

would ever dream of putting aside their hatred and allowing us to return from exile as free men?"

Ben looked at Tom and Joyce. "It would have to be that way."

The commander was groping angrily for words when the mauki spoke for the first time. "There is a more important question to ask," she said softly. She looked up at Ben. "Where do *you* stand? You are the son Ivan Trefon. You carry the name of one of the greatest houses in Spacer history. You know we are at war with the people of Earth; where do you stand now? With us?" Her eyes swept across to Tom Barron and his sister. "Or with them?"

"With them," Ben Trefon said without hesitation.

"And where do *you* stand?" she asked the Barrons. "With your people on Earth? Or with Ben?"

"With Ben," Tom and Joyce Barron said firmly.

"Then what do the three of you want of me?" the mauki asked.

"You've heard why the war must be stopped," Ben said. "We want you to tell the story, to Earthmen and Spacers alike. We know you can make them believe, if you will."

"I see." The woman fell silent, searching each of their faces in turn. Finally her eyes rested on Joyce. "And you were to be a mauki," she said, half smiling. "Would you now?"

Joyce nodded. "If Spacers and Earthmen could both be free."

"And this story you have told me is true?"

"It's true," Joyce Barron said.

"You realize that falsehood and treachery now could destroy your people as well as mine?"

"I know that," Joyce said. "But there is no falsehood and no treachery in this room."

For a long time the mauki stared at her. Then she smiled and turned to the commander. "They're telling the truth," she said. "There is no question of that. The events they speak of happened, and their decision to come to us this way was sound."

"Even so," the commander said, "what can we do?"

"I sang once before because I had a message for the men of Earth," the mauki said. "If enough had heard me then, this war might never have happened. Now they must hear me for sure, before everything is lost." She smiled sadly. "It is painful for children to put away their toys and take up the tools of men. But how much more painful when a child grows up! We no longer dare remain children."

"Then you want to spread this story?" the commander said.

"I do, and the sooner the better. If these young people can find a way to make the others listen."

Perhaps it was the simple fact that none of the Earthmen in the blockading fleet had ever heard a mauki chant before that finally made them agree, from sheer curiosity, to listen.

Of course it was possible that the Earth commander really believed the story that Tom and Joyce told him, although that seemed doubtful when the story was retold in later days. Perhaps he had seen some partisan advantage to it, or perhaps he had already heard of the Spacer fleet poised and ready to move in toward Earth when Ben Trefon piloted his little S-80 back out through the Maze under a flag of truce to bring the Barrons to the command ship.

Whatever his reasons for allowing the truce ship through, the Earth commander was surely suspicious as well as curious. Earthmen through the centuries had heard enough about the strange singing of Spacer women to be cautious of its remarkable power. Rumors and stories had grown over the years; many Earthmen believed that these women the Spacers called maukis had some supernatural gift, some magical power to bend men's wills with the sorcery of their singing. Few Earthmen ever stopped to think that every human civilization since the dawn of history had made music in some form a part of its life, and that in times past other exiled people on Earth itself had developed their own peculiar laments to express themselves.

This had been the way with Spacers. Life in space had never been easy; only through songs and stories could they keep alive the memory of their lives on Earth, and the hopes that they held for returning one day. There was no magic in a mauki chant. It had no mystical power. But always the singing of Spacer women had come from the heart, driven into words by loneliness and longing.

So the Earth commander's fears were empty, but they nearly prevailed nonetheless. When Ben Trefon landed his ship with his Earthling friends in the berth of the great Earth command ship, it was only through the Barrons' insistence that he was allowed to join them in facing the Earth commander at all. And as they recounted the things they had told the commander on Asteroid Central, the Earth commander's face grew heavy with suspicion.

Yet somehow he seemed to sense the urgency in what they were saying. When they finished he regarded them thoughtfully. "So it is to end hostilities that you wish us to hear this mauki sing," he said at last. "Very well, we will agree. Let your commander surrender his fortress to us and order his outlying fleet to disarm. We will grant amnesty to all but your leaders, and make every humane effort to permit you to return to your homes in space. Then we will allow your mauki to sing her message to people on Earth and in space alike, and see if the end of your exile can be negotiated."

Ben's face turned red as he listened; now he shook his head vehemently. "There will be no surrender, conditional or otherwise."

The Earth commander turned to Tom Barron. "You want the woman to sing. Convince your friend to accept my terms."

"Never," Tom Barron said. "The Spacers are not about to surrender. Let the mauki sing first."

"How do we know this is not a trap?" the Earth commander said. "We would have to stop blocking their radios in order to broadcast her message. How can we be sure that a message will not go out ordering the outlying fleet to attack Earth at once? How do we know that the woman won't hypnotize us all with her words?"

"You can't know," Ben Trefon said. "You simply have to take the risk that our word will be good."

The commander looked at him. "Then you must also be willing to take a risk."

"Like what?"

"Like bringing the mauki out to this ship to sing."

"Of course. She will gladly come."

"And you will pilot one of our warships through the Maze to fetch her," the Earth commander said.

Ben's jaw sagged, and he realized with a sinking feeling that he was trapped. One warship, carrying one hydrogen warhead, and Asteroid Central could be destroyed. One blow, dealt in treachery, could be the final blow of the war, triggering mass retaliation from the Spacers' outlying fleet.

"Well?" the Earth commander demanded. "What do you say?"

Ben turned to Tom and drew him aside. "What shall I do?" he said. "What can I tell him?"

"Tell him you accept," Tom said. "Not a shell will be fired if he gives his word. I'm certain of it."

"But you could be wrong."

"If I'm wrong, then everything is lost."

Ben Trefon took a deep breath and turned back to the

Earth commander. If there was treachery, the blame would rest on his shoulders, but it could not be helped. Somewhere, sometime, there had to be a starting place for mutual trust and understanding. "All right," he said. "I'll take your warship through."

Anyone born and raised in space was accustomed to danger, and Ben Trefon had made many perilous journeys before. But never before had he felt the peril so overwhelmingly as he did now as he nosed the great battle cruiser from the Earth fleet into the passage through the Maze heading for Asteroid Central and the mauki who was waiting there.

It had been agreed that Ben would pilot the ship, after he had convinced the Earth commander that experience and navigational skill were as critical to a safe passage as knowledge of the proper route to follow. He had chosen the passage that required the least speed and maneuverability, for the Earth ship was slow and clumsy in its reactions and his own unfamiliarity with the controls was an impediment. Tom Barron was at his side at the control panel, while Joyce waited back on the command ship, but the Earth commander had elected to accompany them, and the cruiser carried a full battle crew of twenty men.

Cautiously Ben eased the ship forward, waiting for the rift in the whirling asteroids to appear that would signal a safe entry into the Maze. He knew that radio silence had been broken long enough to beam a message straight at Asteroid Central's main receivers: HOLD YOUR FIRE! A CONTACT SHIP IS COMING THROUGH! HOLD YOUR FIRE! Earlier he had personally talked for fifteen minutes to the commander on Asteroid Central, his voice carried on a tight beam to prevent Central from broadcasting beyond the blockade. But try as he would, he could not persuade the commander to promise no attack on the great Earth ship. Finally he had broken contact deliberately, hoping that time to reconsider might change his commander's mind.

He could understand the commander's viewpoint, of course. It would be suicide to allow an enemy battleship to penetrate the Maze without some kind of guarantee that Asteroid Central would not be fired upon. All of the Earth commander's assurances that no shell would be fired without provocation would mean very little indeed if one shell were then launched in treachery. And now, try as he would to put them from his mind, he was remembering all the stories he had ever heard of the native inborn treachery and faithlessness of Earthmen when Spacers had been foolish enough to trust them.

However, now the time for trust had finally arrived. Promises would not mend the centuries of distrust between his people and the Earthmen. Sometimes someone had to make himself vulnerable, someone had to be willing to take the risk if there was to be any hope of bringing the Searchers' message to Earthmen and Spacer alike. Ben noticed the tension on the faces of the cruiser's men, and he relaxed a little. There was no sign of elation here, no sign of excitement of an impending victory. The Earth commander was pacing the cabin nervously, watching Ben's every move as though his only concern was that the great missile tubes on Asteroid Central really hold their fire after all.

There was no doubt about it. The commander and crew were as nervous as he was. He edged the ship forward as the rift appeared, and abruptly the great ship was moving deep into the Maze.

It was a slow passage, requiring three complete orbits of Asteroid Central. Ben watched closely as the gaps in the pattern appeared, allowing him to nose the ship in closer and then closer again. He concentrated on the ship's controls, trying to clear his mind of other things. Even trouble in the Maze could be disastrous; if anything should happen to the Earth ship during the passage, the Earth commander would be convinced that Ben had personally sabotaged it. But slowly the great asteroid drew closer, until the surface was clearly visible on the view screen.

Confused activity was everywhere. Two of the main landing ports had opened and the great scanning telescopes were peering up at the approaching ship. Tiny figures of men could be seen manning the fixed missile tubes that flanked the ports like bristling whiskers. Ben could identify the stepwise makeready for attack going on even following the movements at this distance.

Behind him the Earth commander walked to the intercom. "All right, men," he said. "Battle stations. Man every gun and make ready."

The men moved swiftly; one by one the battle stations reported themselves manned and ready. Ben hit the controls sharply, veering the ship out of collision course with a vagrant asteroid fragment and then ducking down into a larger gap that was opening up. Only a few more to go, he thought, and it's up to them.

"Load tubes one and two," the Earth commander said. Ben

felt the hair prickle on the back of his neck, but he kept his attention glued to the controls. Of course they're afraid, he kept telling himself. They've got to be ready, in case the silly fools down there open up on them. He moved the ship into the last gap in the Maze before it could break free for a landing pattern. Suddenly, it was hard for him to breathe. Sweat stood out on his forehead, and beside him he saw Tom Barron gripping the shock bar until his knuckles were white. Another shift, and the ship was free of the Maze.

"Take it down," the Earth commander said.

Below them the great asteroid loomed large, the main landing port gaping open like the jaws of a fantastic monster. There was utter silence in the ship's cabin now; no one was breathing as Ben threw switches and dropped the nose of the cruiser down for the landing port.

At last, miraculously, the ship was down. There was a whir of grappling cables. Ben killed the power and sat back. Nothing happened.

He heard a tense breath expelled behind him, and the Earth commander said, "Now take me in."

Flanked by Ben Trefon and Tom Barron, the Earthman marched up the ramp into the Spacer stronghold. The ramp was lined with Spacers standing with hand weapons ready, their faces tense, their eyes alert for any false move. Passing between them, Ben led the way down the corridor and into the meeting room where he and the Barrons had made their final plans with the mauki.

The Spacer commander and the mauki were waiting, and there was something of wonder on the commander's face as he saw his Earth-born counterpart stop short, salute him, and turn to the woman with a stiff formal bow.

"It is our understanding," the Earth commander said, "that this woman has a message of importance for us all to hear. We have agreed to suspend hostilities until that message has been heard, providing you also cease your fire and control your fleet."

The Spacer commander nodded slowly, staring at Ben as if he could not believe his ears. "You have our pledge."

"Then we request that the woman return with us," the Earthman said. "In return for that concession, we will break our scrambler screen so that your people as well as ours can hear the message."

Once again the Spacer commander nodded. "It is so agreed."

Without another word, the Earth commander turned to the

mauki. He took her arm in an oddly gentlemanly gesture, nodded to Ben and Tom, and turned back toward the Earth ship.

An hour later they returned through the Maze to the Earth command ship. Ten minutes after that the harsh static of the radio scramblers suddenly ceased, and a message went out from Asteroid Central to the outlying fleet ordering Tommy Whisk to stand by without action until further orders.

The message had hardly been acknowledged when silence fell in every Spacer shop and concourse, on every Earth ship, and in all the relay stations that were alerted to pick up the message and carry it back across the millions of miles of space to the powerful receivers on Earth herself.

And then, at last, the mauki began to sing.

EPILOGUE

OF ALL THE stories in Earth's long history probably none was so strange, and none destined to be retold so often and in so many versions as the story of the woman's voice that had ended the Earth-Spacer war and brought to a close the centuries of bitterness between men of the planet and men who dwelt in the outer reaches of the solar system.

Some said the woman sang in English, and others said in Russian. Some said she sang in the native dialect of the Indians of Mexico, or of the Greenland Eskimos; others insisted that her chant had been in the language of the Orient or of the great African nations. But whatever the language, there was agreement on one thing: that of all who heard her sing (and perhaps no message had ever been heard by so many people in so many places at the same time) not one had failed to understand the message she was conveying.

Later, of course, the words were written down in sundry languages for everyone to read and ponder and—ultimately—to understand. It was a story that touched everyone who heard it, for it was a story of the planet Earth, and of the exasperating race of intelligent people who had grown up on her surface, a race of curious and powerful creatures, pulling themselves up by their bootstraps, groping through the centuries to learn how to use the intelligence they possessed. It was a story of enormous accomplishment and of enormous failure.

The mauki's song told the story of the history of those men, sometimes weak, sometimes powerful, sometimes ambitious, sometimes lazy, sometimes subjecting themselves to tyrannical rulers and evil causes, but always ultimately throwing off the yoke in a fierce and relentless independence, always reaching upward and upward with the intelligence of their birthright. She sang of the march of kings and Caesars, of revolutions against tyranny and of the free societies that rose from the ashes of those revolutions. Through her song ran a relentless theme: the driving struggle between good and evil that men had always been engaged in, the struggle between freedom and slavery.

Her song recounted events of history that had long been forgotten as she led her listeners step by step through the Dark Ages and the Renaissance, through the great wars of the twentieth century and the rising tide of scientific advances that took men into space. Finally she sang of the mortal struggle that had arisen out of the Spacer conspiracy and now had reached its climax in this present war between Earthmen and Spacers.

And then the mauki sang of the future. In measured strains that could not be mistaken she sang of the crooked road that men had followed since the exile of the Spacers had begun and the direction in which it inevitably led: to certain destruction, to the crippling of the race and the wasting of its intelligence, perhaps to obliteration of life on the planet altogether. But she sang of another future that could be, in which men had ceased fighting each other and turned their energies toward the enormous achievements of which they were capable. No one who heard her could mistake the message of the Searchers which she passed on—the grim warning on the one hand, the promise of greatness on the other. As the last words of the mauki's chant faded into silence, there was no one who heard her who could question the alternative to be chosen.

Of course the changes would not come about overnight. No one pretended to expect that. Old hatreds still flared. Old fears still paralyzed the thinking of many men. The end of suspicions that had festered for centuries would not be brought about by magic, and the wise ones both on Earth and in space acknowledged that decades and maybe centuries would be required to heal the wounds laid raw by human childishness.

But now, at least, there was a reason to try.

In the first days after the blockade was broken Ben Trefon returned to Earth with the two friends who had stood by his side when the mauki chant began. Before, he came as a raider. Now he came in peace, as an envoy from the Spacer Council, to help in the vast job of education and change that had to be done. Soon after their return Joyce Barron went back to her training in nursing in a Chicago hospital, but Ben and Tom continued their tour of the cities and nations of Earth, working as a team to build and reinforce the strength of the Searchers' message.

But Ben Trefon was first and last a Spacer. Presently the oppressive atmosphere, the difference in gravity and the pressing crowds of people at every hand became more than he could bear, and he made ready to return to Asteroid Central.

He was not surprised to learn that Tom Barron was returning with him, one of the first Earthmen to be accepted for training in the school of space navigation on Asteroid Central.

"I hope you realize what you're buying into," Ben warned his friend on the night of their departure. "Life out there won't be easy just because we have peace and free access to Earth. Space will always be a hard master, and men in space will still carry the flaw they have always carried. There are still no girls born in space."

Tom Barron nodded. "I know. At least not now; some of our geneticists think that a solution can be found, and that soon there won't even be that distinction between Earthmen and Spacers. And I'm not looking for an easy life, exactly."

"But you had work to do down here."

"There are plenty here to do it," Tom replied. "Plenty and more than plenty. For me, I know as well as you do where the important work is waiting to be done."

They stood on the wide upper concourse above the vast residential city where the Barrons' quarters were located. Over their heads the sky was dark, and a night wind filtered across the city. Tom walked to the guard railing, staring at the sky. "It looks different here," he said. "With the skyglow and the thick atmosphere, you'd never dream the number of stars that are out there."

"They're there, all right," Ben agreed.

"And some day fleets of ships will be going out. That will be where the real work begins, when the Searchers come back."

"Maybe," Ben Trefon said, but he knew Tom Barron was right. Some day the time would come. But for now, strangely enough, the Searchers had disappeared. Since the night the mauki had sung her song, Spacer and Earth ships together had combed the solar system in search of the small gray men with the misty-blue eyes, but no sign of them had been found. Whether they had really left the solar system altogether, or were simply hiding and watching as they had watched before, nobody knew. Some even questioned that they had ever been there at all, but Ben Trefon still wore the black web belt around his waist, with the shiny capsule lodged in its pocket.

Now he touched the metallic surface lightly and felt the barely perceptible vibration that was there.

"They'll be back," he said confidently. "Some day, when the time is right, we'll meet them again."

Tom grinned at his Spacer friend. "Let's be honest. They'll be back when we're ready for them, and not a minute before. But who knows? That may be sooner than we think."

Side by side they crossed the glittering concourse and started down the ramp toward the space port.